What Price Glory?
A Civil War Collection

Nick Korolev

WORDWOOZE
PUBLISHING

Wordwooze Publishing
wordwooze.com

Also by Nick Korolev

The Swamp Dragon
Dark Waters
Lucky Nat: Justice for a Slaver
Ghost of a Chance
The 13th Child
Arizona Red Ghost
Flashback: Life After Murder
The Cat Who Fell to Earth

To Richard "Byrdie" Byrd and our mutual friend John Brindle who has answered the last bugle call and all those who teach through living history.

Foreword

Historical fiction is a genre that usually conjures up images of a romantic story set in a long-ago time. But there is another part of the genre, a story about real history where characters are caught up in the drama of the time, be they fictional or real people or a mixture of both. This collection of historical fiction is of the latter type and will take the reader on a journey into the most tragic time in US history—the Civil War.

Arranged along a rough timeline when they took place, these short stories and one novella cover a broad area of mood and events. They run from a young man's escape from an outlaw gang in Missouri to join a North Carolina regiment back home (*The Journey*), to the discovery of Lee's lost orders by a Union sergeant (*Three Cigars*), to a boy too curious about war (*To See the Elephant*), to a young woman who has dressed like a man to join her brother in the war (*Amazon*), and to two enemies who become friends over a fishing hole (*The Great Mudbug War*). Also, there are two stories about iconic leaders, Stonewall Jackson (*The Last Battle*) and Colonel Joshua L. Chamberlain (the novella *The Crucible*). And one story is told by General Sheridan's horse, Rienzi, of the famous ride that turned the tide at Cedar Creek (*Rienzi: Right from the Horse's Mouth*).

It is my hope the reader will enjoy this bit of time travel that puts flesh on the bones of history and perhaps learn a little more of this tragic time that separated people to help stop the same kind of divide happening in our country today.

The Journey

Nettles, Missouri was a one-horse town without a horse. William Spencer sat in his upstairs room at the Rosebud Hotel looking out an open window at the dusty main street in the failing light of day. The Wild Goose Saloon across the way was doing a brisk business by the sound of it.

The Oak Creek Gang, his gang, was over there; Sam Clayton, the leader whose cruel eyes missed nothing; Jeff Crawford, whipcord hard and quick with a Colt; Nat Lance, quiet and built like a bull with just as mean a temper—all of them no doubt drinking and whoring.

But he did not feel like celebrating. He could not glory in killing a man. He was just eighteen, lanky, with a thick thatch of unruly brown hair and brown eyes, and an inch shy of six feet. The outlaw life he had thought would be easy money had chewed him up and spit him out. He could not tell the others of his change of heart. They were not the kind of men who took such things lightly. The gang sometimes rode with Quantrill, a notorious bushwhacker who regarded anyone with Union sympathies as fair game. If he dared to speak his mind on his present feelings, they would simply consider him a risk and kill him. Right now, they just thought supper did not agree with him. He sighed and leaned back in the wood chair.

No matter what he tried to think about, all he could see was his Arkansas toothpick sticking out between the ribs of the well-dressed man who had moments before stepped off the stagecoach. Jeff had made fast work of the driver and guard, who lay bleeding in the road. The other passengers, two men and a woman, were too scared to react in a hostile manner. It was a stage holdup gone bad as far as he was concerned.

He closed his eyes tightly to squeeze out the vision. He shook his head. "For God sakes, Will, he pulled a derringer," he said in a North Carolina drawl. "You was justified. It was him or you."

It was pure instinct and cat-quick reflexes that had his hand reaching for the big knife in the back of his belt as the man began to pull the gun from a pocket when he was supposedly reaching for a billfold. Will knew the wide-eyed look of surprise on the man's face as the weapon fell from his hand, and the blood slowly spreading on his silk vest would be with him forever.

He got up and went over to the bed, turned the oil lamp on the small table next to it to a lower flame, creating a dull glow on the whitewashed walls of the small room. He stretched out on the bed to think. He had to do something about his situation and fast. His cut from the holdup was $250, a sum that could get him anyplace he wanted to go by train or stage if he could get to one in a bigger town. At this point he wanted to put as many miles as possible between himself and the Oak Creek Gang.

Home to Ames Crossing, North Carolina was not on his list of options. He had ended up in this mess fleeing a miserable home life two years ago. His father, Curtis Spencer, was an abusive drunk and often beat him, his mother, Anna, and older sister, Mary. His mother had the good sense to run off after Mary got married to a wealthy planter from out near Raleigh. He stayed another few months taking double the abuse, then ran away and caught a boxcar West in the summer.

He was thrown off the train near Ducktown just across the Tennessee border. He spent the night in an abandoned barn. From there he walked to Chattanooga, where he took on a job as an assistant clerk at Bailey's General Store. The owner, Jacob Bailey, was a kind and fair man. His seventeen-year-old daughter, Amy, with strawberry blonde hair and green eyes, was a beauty beyond

2

his wildest dreams. She turned every young man's head in town. The job was good, an honest job. He made enough to stay in a local hotel with money to spare. But he was there for only four months. He got himself emotionally entangled with Amy and left the night she told him she was pregnant. He was not ready to settle down and felt trapped. He got on a train to Columbus, Kentucky and decided to go as far West as his savings would take him. He took a stage to the next railhead and bought a ticket to St. Louis. It was there that he met Sam Clayton. Now he was paying for his wandering ways.

Pistol shots and whoops brought him instantly to the window. Men were spilling out of the Wild Goose in a festive mood. Sam, Jeff, and Nat were among them.

When Jeff and Nat crossed the street to below his window, he shouted down to them, "What the hell is this all about?"

Jeff yelled up, "Well, if you wasn't a' holed up in your room..."

Nat cut in, "A feller brought in the St. Louis newspaper. Seem's we're beatin' the Yanks in the East. Jackson's pounding them good in the Shenandoah, and they're saying we'll probably have Washington by the end of summer!"

The news stunned him. He'd be the first to admit he did not follow events reported in the papers. He didn't give two hoots for politics, the rebellion, or anything that was happening outside his personal world. He only cared about the basics of survival: food and shelter, money to spend, and a good roll in the hay with a willing country girl now and then. He certainly felt no compulsion to take sides in a conflict that now seemed to be turning serious.

"Come and join us for a celebration," Sam called, holding up a bottle of whiskey as he crossed the street.

"Yeah, a little drink will do you good. Don't be such a wet blanket, Will," Nat added.

"I ain't feelin' so good. Head's pounding like someone was hittin' it with a sledge, and my belly ain't much better. Don't want

3

to spend the rest of the night pukin' my guts out," he yelled down. "I'm goin' back to bed. See you in the mornin'."

He turned away from the window as more shots were fired at the night sky. There was so much whooping, hollering, and shooting, he would have sworn it was the Fourth of July or a battle raging in the street.

Then a thought struck. Now would be the perfect time to escape this bad turn in his life. The Oak Creek Gang would be too hungover in the morning to follow him.

He went directly to his saddlebags and checked to make sure the cash was still there. Then he stepped to the door and listened. All he could hear was the racket in the street behind him. He snatched up his saddlebags and stepped into the hall, lit dully by an oil lamp on the stained wall. On a whim, he visited each empty room of the gang and took what cash he found still in their saddlebags. Then he headed for the back stairs but found the door to them locked. He paused.

"Damn," he muttered. "The hell with it."

He kicked it open and quickly climbed down the steep wooden back stairs, knowing no one heard him over the celebration. Using the hotel and general store next door as cover, he jogged through the night shadows to the back of the livery stable. The back door was locked. He went in along the side, stopping at the corner in the shadows of a massive chestnut tree to peek out at the main street.

He spotted Jeff and Sam sharing the bottle. Sam drank the last of it, then threw it in the air and blasted it to smithereens with his Colt.

Will ducked back around the corner, his heart hammering. He froze, listening to more hollering and shouting. He was only ten feet from the open stable door just around the corner. But if Jeff or Sam spotted him, there'd be hell to pay. He held his breath and looked around the corner again. The Oak Creek Gang was headed back to the saloon with other revelers, Sam quite unsteady on his feet.

He bolted around the corner through the shadows and into the stable. A lit lamp was on a desk in a corner box stall that served as an office. The owner, Mr. Pearson, a big burly man with a shaved head, was repairing a harness. There was no way he could sneak by the man, so he went directly to him. "Sir, how much do I owe you?" he asked boldly.

Pearson looked up from his work. "A dollar. You leaving town?"

"Yep." He did not feel like explaining any more. He dug in his pocket and pulled out a silver dollar.

"Your mare is in the third stall down on the right," Pearson said, eyeing him suspiciously.

"Your friends know you're leaving?"

He walked to the black mare without answering. She nickered a greeting as she always did. He patted her rump to get her to move so he could reach the lead rope. She was stolen property, but he no longer cared. Sam had given her to him instead of cash from the robbery of a horse trader they ambushed with Quantrill on his first job six weeks ago. She was one of a small herd of horses that was supposed to be delivered to the Union Army. The mare had been a weedy thing but had filled out since then. She could run like the wind. He named her Raven.

He saddled and bridled her quickly and secured the saddlebags behind the saddle under his blanket roll. Then he rode out into the night at a gallop, turning sharply to the right, away from the saloon, Raven's hooves striking sparks on a few stones in the road. He never wanted to see Nettles, Missouri or the Oak Creek Gang again.

Once he swam Raven across the Mississippi River and entered Tennessee three days later with no sign of the Oak Creek Gang, he began to relax. He spent a whole day lolling on the east bank of the river under ancient cottonwoods, fishing with line he kept in his saddlebags and worms he found under logs for bait. It was an activity he loved, and it gave him time to think and dream. He was not sure what he wanted to do with his life at present.

He looked out at the leaves drifting in the sluggish current of the broad river, thinking that his life had so far meandered with the same aimlessness. It had never bothered him before. He reasoned it only bothered him now because of the type of men he'd been hanging around with the last few months. Men whose future was a bullet or a hangman's noose. He would not go back to that kind of life. He wanted something better. But what?

A fish hit his line. It was heavy and pulled so hard it almost made the line cut into his hands. It took him a while to pull it in … a nice fat catfish. *At least I won't go hungry tonight or be forced to raid a local hen house.* Then he went about making a campfire using driftwood he found along the river. After he finished eating, he added a few thick branches to the fire and fell asleep.

When Raven snorted, Will sat bolt upright, suddenly alert. The first thought that entered his mind was that the Oak Creek Gang had found him. His hand reached for the big knife in his belt. He called out, "Who's there?"

There was no answer, only something moving through the brush. He wished he had purchased a pistol, like Sam had told him to. It could be a deer, or it could be a man out there.

"You better show yourself or I'll start shooting," he bluffed. "I ain't in no mood for foolin' around."

"All right," came a reedy voice. "I wasn't sure you was friendly."

"Who said I am?" he shot back. "I don't like fellows sneaking around my camp. Came out of Missouri where it ain't safe."

"Well, it ain't much safer here in Tennessee with them damn Yankees all over. You going to sign up?"

"Come close so I can see you, or I ain't answerin' any more of your questions."

6

A youth about his own age, dressed in rough clothes and slouch hat like himself, came out of the dark into the feeble fringe of the campfire light. He was well-built with blond hair and innocent brown eyes.

"Sit down over there where I can see you."

The youth moved closer to the fire directly across from Will. The boy was unarmed. "I'm Jed Hulsey from Corning, Arkansas," the youth said. "I'm on my way to Union City to visit my sister and her new husband before I join up."

"I'm Will Spencer from Ames Crossing, North Carolina. Union City's kind of a long walk from here, ain't it?"

"Well, I started out riding, but my horse went lame, and I had to leave it in Blytheville. Was going to catch the stage at Dyersburg not far from here if it's still running."

"Well, you can ride double with me. Raven can carry us both. What's all this about signing up?"

"You been livin' in a cave? There's a shooting war on. Has been for some time. The damn Yankees telling us we can't be a free country. They've invaded the South. They're right here in Tennessee."

"Oh, that," he said, leaning back against his saddle. "It ain't none of my concern."

"The Federal government a comin' to your state to tell you at gunpoint how to live, stealin' your food and livestock, and maybe even rapin' your womenfolk ain't none of your concern?"

"No one's run my life since I left home. Why should I worry about some Federal troops that ain't nowhere near?"

"'Cause it ain't right. We're whippin' them good in the East, though. Only problem is there's more of them than there is of us. I figure if as many of us as can go an' get involved now, they may get tired of fighting and all go home."

Will burst out laughing. Jed looked quite offended, and that made Will laugh all the harder to the point of tears. When he finally got control, he went on. "You want to go out there and get shot because the Federal army has come South to put down your rebellion, you go right ahead."

"I don't plan to get shot. I plan to shoot as many of them as I can."

Will sat up. "Jed, you're just plum crazy. You'll probably get yourself killed."

"Well, if I do, I'll die doing something right. I'll die doing something for the good of my family and country. Don't you care about nobody but yourself?"

The words stung and made him want to plant his fist in that innocent face. "I care. I care about livin' and doin' something else with my life besides throwin' it away in some dumbass war."

"What are you goin' to do with your life? Huh?" Jed's tone was harsh, demanding.

Will frowned. He was just a muscle twitch away from beating up this fool for challenging him. "I don't know. But it ain't none of your business. I don't answer to you. Besides, I bet you ain't ever killed a man. I have. So, shut your mouth and go to sleep. We got a long day of ridin' tomorrow." He settled back on his saddle and pulled the blanket up against the river chill.

"Maybe I ain't tired," Jed retorted.

"Well, I am. If you ain't, you can go fetch some more driftwood for the fire, if you've a mind to."

"I might just do that," Jed said.

Will rolled over and watched him leave the camp, not quite trusting him. Jed headed toward the river. Satisfied his companion was as innocent as he seemed, Will dropped off to sleep.

Will woke before dawn, anxious to get started. Jed was missing. *Good. I can travel quicker alone and don't have to put up with Jed's patriotic lectures.* He was just saddling Raven when Jed turned up with a couple of catfish.

8

"Can't travel on an empty stomach. Found your line by the fire where you cleaned a fish last night." He grinned.

"Well, seein' it's likely to be our last meal for a while, let's get them in the fire," he said, tightening the girth.

He kept the saddlebags close to him as he got the fire going. Jed gutted the fish and put them on sticks. They ate looking out at the sluggish Mississippi. He wondered for a moment what Jed was thinking about. Then his thoughts wandered, getting lost in the ever-changing eddies and whirlpools of the muddy water.

Jed's annoying voice interrupted his reverie. "You'll have to stay for dinner when we get to my sister's place. One taste of her chicken and you'll think you've died and gone to heaven."

There was a distant rumble. Thunder on a clear spring day? Jed's head snapped around to listen. The rumble came again, sounding like more of a thump.

"Jesus! That's artillery, and it's on our side of the river," Jed announced. Sounds like it's almost where we have to go."

It thumped again against the distant green horizon and gave Will a jumpy feeling in his stomach. The truth hit with it, a truth he had been ignoring for months. As much as he hated to admit it, the Yankees were not far away. Suddenly, he felt as if this war of Jed's was closing in on him. If he wasn't careful, it would smother him.

"Damn," he said, then looked at Jed. "Finish up and let's git."

In moments, they were riding double on Raven. They headed east away from the river, cutting across pasture and around the edge of a cornfield, the young plants hardly a foot tall. Then they found a road.

"Go left," was all Jed said.

Will turned the mare and clucked gently at her. She moved out at a fast walk.

Finally, Jed spoke again. "I hope the damn Yankees ain't in Union City."

Will said nothing. He became more uneasy with every passing mile. His eyes darted to the leaves stirring in the shadows of the spring-green landscape. A movement became advancing troops. A fleeing deer became a mounted officer. His growing anxiety began to telegraph itself to Raven. The black mare's ears were flicking back and forth, and she sniffed the air.

He was watching the shifting shadows in a thick wood lot on his left as they came around a bend in the road. Jed shouted in his ear, "Cavalry! Yankee cavalry ahead!"

He looked. The road ahead was as straight as a rifle shot. The mounted bluecoats were about a quarter mile away. They moved at a steady pace, showing no sign of noticing the black mare and her riders.

"Jesus!" he breathed and headed Raven into the woods at a jolting trot, with Jed hanging on so tight around his chest he could hardly breathe. They plunged into the cool green shadows under tall oaks into a small fern-filled clearing. Will hauled the horse to a stop and turned to Jed. "You best get off here and hide," he said. "Raven can't carry the two of us far at any speed."

"You leavin' me here?" Jed's eyes were wild with fear.

"You know these parts better'n me. You'll be all right."

"You … damn coward." Will felt Jed go after the big knife in his belt. Instantly, he swung around sharply, elbowing Jed hard in the head, knocking him right off the mare. "No one calls me a coward or tries to kill me with my own knife!" he yelled, putting his heels to the mare.

They flew across the clearing into the woods.

"I hope a Yankee gets you! You yellow bastard!" Jed spat.

He had no idea where he was going, only *that* he was going. He guided the mare at a swift trot deeper into the forest, dodging around trees. Soon, he lost all sense of direction in the undergrowth of bullbriers and wild grapevines. Suddenly, he began to hear voices, the clank of equipment, and horses. It quickly pushed him to the

10

verge of panic. He reined in the mare, his heart pounding. Through the dense tangle of vegetation ahead he saw shadows moving. Then he realized he must have doubled back in his confusion, or perhaps the road made a sharp turn through the woods. He dared not move and hoped a trooper would not come poking around the brush that hid him from the road. They would think him a spy or bushwhacker and probably hang him, he told himself.

Only when the sounds of the moving column of horsemen recede did he breathe easier. He edged Raven closer to the road through the tangle of grapevines. The path looked empty. He decided to wait a few more moments before venturing into the open. He was not in a rush to get shot at.

The whole experience sobered him. He wondered if it was a patrol or an invasion force. He suddenly felt foolish not paying attention to the wider world around him over the past few months. A seed of anger sprouted within him. How dare these troops keep him from using a public road. *Fool. I wouldn't have a chance if they stopped me and found the knife.*

Raven nickered. He heard the soft tread of hooves on the forest floor behind him and started to turn.

"Don't you move a muscle, boy," a low voice sounded behind him.

He froze.

"There's still more coming," the voice continued. A lanky man with a week's growth of beard pulled next to him on a bay horse. He was wearing a short gray shell jacket with a yellow collar and a line of gold braid on the sleeves. His blue trousers were tucked into knee-high boots. A pair of Colt pistols was strapped to his waist. A slouch hat, pulled low, shaded his eyes.

"God, you gave me a fright," Will said quietly, trying not to let the man see his hands were shaking.

11

The man looked at him and Raven in an appraising manner. "You ain't from around here, are you?" the man asked in a low voice.

"No, I ain't."

"Thought as much by the way you went meandering through these woods. Where you headed?"

"Anywhere away from here."

"Well, if I'm right, the Yanks are on the move. The area is full of cavalry patrols."

"Who are you?"

"Lieutenant Charles Forsythe with Forrest's cavalry. I'm on my way back from a short leave. I live about ten miles south of here. Just got off the road in time and picked up your trail."

"Oh," he said and decided to be truthful. "I don't rightly know where I'm headed. I'm from North Carolina. Came from Missouri. Decided the West weren't for me."

"Well, if you've got a mind to return there, you'd better go by way of Georgia and try to get a train north if you're in a rush. If you plan on joining the army to run off these damn invaders, you can come with me. I'm sure Forrest could use you."

"Much obliged for the information. As to joinin' the army … if I decide to, it will be a unit from North Carolina. No offense."

Forsythe gave him a skeptical look. "No offense taken. Forrest's cavalry ain't for everyone. We ride fast and he drives us hard. Your mare's a skinny little thing and might not be able to take it. You're welcome to ride with me as far as you want."

Will considered the wisdom of Forsythe's offer. Since he did not know the country or have a map, he thought it a good idea. "I'll take you up on your offer."

They fell silent at the approach of another column of blue cavalry. They waited a good while after the troops passed before they headed out to the road. As they rode away from the woods, Will

12

wondered only briefly what became of the pest, Jed. Then he gave him no more thought.

He found Forsythe a pleasant companion for the two days they traveled together. The lieutenant kept him entertained with stories about the cavalry and his escape with Forrest from Fort Donaldson on a snowy dawn back in February. Forsythe spoke of the crossing of an icy backwater of the Cumberland River, many of the men carrying behind their saddles infantrymen who refused to surrender. He was amazed that despite the snow, cold, biting wind, and sheer exhaustion, Forrest and his men covered the seventy-five miles to Nashville in just two days.

As he listened to more of Forsythe's adventures, Will's thoughts shifted. Always resentful of authority and those in his life who tried to force it down his throat like his brutal father, he began to sympathize with the South against the Northern aggressor. The seed of anger and resentment that had sprouted was now fed by a desire to become involved. That desire became an obsession to get to North Carolina and find a regiment he could join.

When the time came to part ways, Will felt sadness he was not accustomed to. Forsythe looked him straight in the eye as they shook hands. "You take care, Will. Watch your back even amongst your own kind. You'll find all types of men in the army who joined for all sorts of reasons. Some ain't much better than a common thief."

"I will. You take care yourself," he said and swallowed hard.

Then Forsythe turned his bay away and headed down a lane off the main road. Will watched him until he was out of sight. He never felt so alone in his life.

Avoiding the main roads where he could, Will traveled parallel to them or on country lanes, asking directions of the people he met. Many who found out where he was going and why asked him to join them for supper. On those days he got a good meal, and Raven got to graze and a treat of oats or corn.

13

He did not go by way of Georgia. He took his chances and headed due east across Tennessee through open farmland and mountains. Four days after he left Forsythe, he crossed the Tennessee River just north of Chattanooga. He avoided the city but not the bittersweet memories of Amy, the feel and smell of her against his body. He caught a train at Cleveland and stayed in a boxcar with Raven, ready to bolt at the sign of bluecoats. The train was slow, stopping frequently at the least threat of a problem up the line, but it still covered far more ground in less time than he could on horseback. He got off at Johnson City, bought some food, and headed southeast to the mountains.

The wild and beautiful Appalachian Mountains, where spring mists rose and hung in clouds in the hollows, soon spread out before him as far as he could see. There he could lose himself from the war for a while. He rode through meadows filled with brilliant wildflowers and followed deer trails through thickets of blooming mountain laurel and rhododendrons.

In four days of marathon travel by horse and rail, he reached Weldon, North Carolina and stopped. Weldon was a small town not far from the North Carolina–Virginia border. The Weldon–Petersburg Railroad ran north from there. His cousin, Frank Spencer, had a farm on the outskirts of town. It was there that he headed rather than Raleigh, where his sister lived on a huge plantation. His reason was simple. He had not seen her since she married John Taylor, and he doubted she would recognize him in his ruffian attire. And there would be too many questions he did not want to answer.

He rode down the narrow lane through an apple orchard toward the modest wood-and-shingle farmhouse. He found Frank's wife, Clara, shelling peas on the front porch. He whistled and waved, then yelled, "Clara! Clara, it's me, Will."

She looked up, hastily set aside the bowl, and ran down the porch stairs. "Will!"

14

He put Raven into a canter and caught up to Clara quickly. "Will, I can't believe it's you! Frank will be so surprised," she said, stopping.

He dismounted. "Where is he?"

"He took the bay mare to the Conner's stallion to be bred. He should be back soon. Will you join us for supper?"

"Thank you, Clara, I certainly will. And if it won't be puttin' you out none, I'd like to stay a couple of days."

"We'll be glad to have you. I'll fix up the spare room. What brings you to Weldon?" She picked up the bowl of peas and headed into the house.

He tied the mare's reins to the porch rail and followed her into the modest parlor furnished with a couch, rocker, and Queen Anne chair. "Well, I plan on joinin' the army and gettin' involved in this war. I ain't got nothin' better to do."

She turned to him sharply at the kitchen entrance, almost spilling the peas. "Will, you?" She sighed. "You have your whole life ahead of you. What put that notion in your head?"

"A lot has happened since I saw you at my sister's wedding. I've been all the way to Missouri. I seen a lot of things, some not so pleasant. They got me to thinking I should get involved. Help get the damn Yankees out of our lands. It ain't right Federal troops comin' here to tell us how to live … you know?"

She put the bowl down on an oak table. "I suppose it might do you some good to join the army. Young men your age need direction. But don't you dare try to convince Frank to go with you. I can't manage this farm alone." She went to a cupboard and took out some clean linen. On her way to a small room off the kitchen she said, "I'm in a family way with our first child."

"Oh," he said. "But you know if Frank has a mind to, he will join."

"Hopefully, not when he finds out he's going to be a father."

15

He followed her, stopping at the doorway to watch her make the bed. "He don't know about the baby yet?"

"I'm going to tell him tonight."

"Well, I can keep a secret."

She smiled at him, her blue eyes twinkling. "You go put your mare up in the barn and feed her. She looks like she could use a good rest. Where 'bouts did you come from?"

"Missouri … all the way in from Missouri."

"My Lord, you both could use the rest and good food." Her words shadowed him as he left the house.

He saw to it that Raven was comfortable in the large stone barn surrounded by three large paddocks with eight fine horses in them. As he headed back toward the house through a scattering of chickens, he spotted Frank, tall and muscular, riding up through the orchard leading a mare. Frank noticed him, suddenly took his slouch hat off and waved it, trotting the horses into the barnyard.

"Will, I ain't seen you in a coon's age." Frank jumped off the gelding, shook hands and hugged him as they pounded each other's backs.

"How've you been doin'?" Will asked.

"Can't complain. My horse breeding program has been doing all right, and we manage to keep ourselves fed and comfortable. What have you been up to?"

"Went west to Missouri, but it didn't agree with me, so I've come back."

"Well, you picked the wrong time. There's a war on."

"I know. I've decided to join up. Nothing else is going on for me right now."

"I'd go myself, but I have too much responsibility right here. So, unless the bluecoats show up at my door, I ain't goin' anywhere."

"Well, I'll do the fighting for both of us then," he said and grinned.

16

The evening passed pleasantly and was made more joyful by Clara's announcement. He and Frank shared some glasses of home-brewed applejack to celebrate. Will had the best night's sleep in weeks on a soft feather mattress.

The next morning after helping Frank with the chores, Will rode into Weldon to have a look around. As he went past the train station, he noticed an army officer walking along the platform carrying a carpetbag with a sword strapped to it. He was a good-looking man of medium height and build who sported a full mustache. Will thought now was as good a time as any to ask some questions about how to join up. He headed Raven over to him. "Sir ... Sir, could you hold up a minute? Got a question."

The officer paused and looked up at him. "How can I help you?"

"Sir, I want to join a North Carolina outfit. How do I go about it?"

"Well, this is your lucky day," he replied with a forced grin. "I am here to recruit more men for the 18th North Carolina. We were hit hard at Seven Days. Lost half our strength. I'll be setting up at the Perkins and Son Law Offices. You come back tomorrow and I'll sign you up. Bring any of your friends who has a mind to join. Oh, by the way, you'll have to sell your mare. The 18th is an infantry unit. If you want to join the cavalry ..."

"No, sir. Your regiment will be fine. Don't want to wait. I want to git in there and git shooting Yankees soon as I can. My name is Will Spencer, sir."

"Well, Mr. Spencer, I appreciate you joining."

"I'll see you tomorrow, sir." He turned the mare and trotted off, knowing at last his life had direction. Where he ended up was in the hands of God, and in his case, he hoped it was a merciful God, considering what he'd done with his life so far.

Three Cigars

It was one of those September mornings that felt more like midsummer, with a lazy warm breeze teasing leaves hardly showing autumn gold. Crickets still chirped in the brush as the 27th Indiana Infantry roused itself before dawn with the rest of the XII Corps and began marching westward toward Frederick, Maryland. To the clank and clatter of equipment and shuffling tread of hundreds of feet, the regiment passed the familiar William Clay and William Hoffman homes in Bartonsville and marched through the area of small deserted cabins they had occupied the winter before. Word had it that the bulk of Lee's army had been in Frederick until just recently, and they might run into enemy cavalry or outposts.

Young First Sergeant John Bloss of Company F, trim with short hair and mustache, squinted at the cabins, noting he always felt secure there, but he sensed that the sudden violent shifts in the fortunes of war were about to change the situation. He had been lucky so far. Very lucky. How much longer could it last? He knew others in line shared the same dismal thoughts. It was as much a part of being a soldier as the uniform they wore.

"What you thinking about, Sergeant?" Corporal Barton Mitchell asked, turning to him as they marched side by side. His normally clean-shaven face was covered with a few days' growth of thin peach fuzz.

"Just reminiscing some about our snug little cabins over yonder," he said.

"These fond memories of yours include the smoke, ague, and blood-sucking graybacks?" Private David Vance cracked from the other side of Mitchell.

18

"Or George's odious nocturnal emissions?" Private John Campbell added behind him and started to laugh hysterically.

George Welsh, the victim marching next to him, pulled his forage cap off and hit him with it several times. "It's the damned food, and you ain't no rose, either."

"All right, Grumble Guts. I surrender," Campbell said, holding up his arm to fend off the playful blows.

"Enough, children," Bloss said, doing his best to stifle a laugh. After all, what respect could he demand as a commander if he broke up at the privates' antics? Command, he had always found, was a rather lonesome place. As a sergeant he stood in the no-man's-land between the enlisted men and the officers, who always acted as the uneasy liaison between the two seeing that orders were followed. He would be in charge of the company if and when the lieutenants and captain were out of action, and he hoped that day would never come.

He glanced ahead at the clean-shaven twenty-two-year-old Captain Kop on foot at the head of the company. The captain's attention was on orders suddenly being shouted down the line. Because their regiment knew the area, they were to form the corps skirmish line as the advance continued between Urbana and New Market.

To the shouts and cajoling of the officers, the regiment spread out across the fields and woods in a loose double line a hundred yards from the main body of the corps. Then they moved out, muskets loaded and held at the ready, tall grass swishing past their legs with brush snapping and crackling under foot, to the clatter of loose equipment. They were too noisy to sneak up on anyone. But that wasn't really the point of this exercise.

"Don't know why the brass don't make the cavalry do this work," Welsh griped. It was an old complaint.

"'Cause the cavalry are scouts, not skirmishers," Campbell shot back.

19

"Well, if things get too tough, we can always feed George here some beans and pork and aim him at the Rebs," Vance added, getting an evil look from Welsh.

"Will you boys just quit and put that to rest? The joke's getin' old," Welsh groused.

Bloss paid little attention to the good-natured exchange. He could see no humor in their situation. His heart pounded. He never relished the easy targets every man on the skirmish line became on open ground, spread so far from each other. After all, their single purpose was to provide an early warning to the rest of the massive column behind them. Any time now they could connect with the enemy, and the bloodshed would start again, beginning with the skirmishers going down. *We are all sacrificial lambs.*

His thoughts got darker. Everyone in the army from generals to lowly privates were all sacrificial lambs so some idiot politicians could make a point. Especially the hotheads in the South like that fanatic John C. Calhoun his pa used to complain about before the war started. Don't get distracted or you'll become a victim of the idiots, he chastised himself.

He grew acutely aware of every bit of cover around him, where every man in his company was walking. He stared ahead at the trees and brush until his eyes hurt from the sun's glare, searching for the first hint of an enemy sniper, the first glint of the sun off a musket barrel. He felt the sun on his head right through the wool of his beat-up kepi. A bead of sweat ran down his back under his stained white shirt and his open dusty blue wool coat. His palms became slick against the wood stock of his musket. This day was quickly becoming as hot as July. He wondered how many in his company would end up casualties of the heat before they even saw a Reb.

"Tally Ho!" some joker yelled from the ranks down the line when a red fox bolted from the cover of an overgrown fence row.

Bloss jumped and hoped no one saw him. Then he watched the fox run in leaping bounds until it disappeared in a thick stand of woods and underbrush.

He could hear a river beyond the trees. He was not thrilled when they reached the knee-deep Monocacy River. He hated marching in wet feet, but the officers did not give anyone much of a chance to take off their shoes.

"Too much of a goddamned rush," he mumbled to himself as they began wading across at Crum's Ford two miles from Frederick. With the cold water creeping up his legs, he found himself begrudging once again the higher-ranking officers on horseback above the wet and muck of the real world of the infantrymen. He splashed across quickly and was thankful when the water did not get above his knees. But at least it cooled him some. He had to be thankful for small blessings.

Several men around him slipped on slick rocks and went down cursing as they struggled up the bank. The smell of wet wool was added to sweat and dust. They fanned out through the woods down the river to the south, searching, probing, daring any hidden enemy to reveal themselves. Nothing.

They turned back toward the city. Bloss and Company F quickly found themselves in the vanguard of the whole army. They were now rapidly reaching the suburbs, where the converging lines of the other companies caused the officers to start calling, "Halt."

"Company, halt!" Bloss echoed the order as his line reached a clover field. They stopped several hundred yards above the river and a hundred yards east of the Georgetown Pike to Washington, not far from where he remembered the Baltimore and Ohio spur from Frederick intersected the main line.

There were signs all around, from garbage dumps to old horse manure, that told the area had been recently occupied by a large force, undoubtedly the Confederates they were searching for. The weary Hoosiers slumped to the ground in the shade on a relatively unspoiled grassy hill near a rail fence and bushes, shedding knapsacks and equipment.

Bees buzzed lazily in the sweet-smelling clover. If he closed his eyes, he could half convince himself he was back home. The peace of it all begged Bloss to relax. He dropped to the ground and put his musket to one side, intent on taking a nap while the officers sorted things out. He noted he was on the right of Corporal Mitchell, with Private Vance lying next to him on the left. Behind to the right of him, Private William Hostetter of Company A lounged on his side, easily recognizable by his flowing mustache.

"Too bad they never leave anything of value behind," Hostetter said, opening his canteen and taking a long drink.

"Well, manure is good fertilizer," Campbell cracked.

"Wonder who exactly was camping here. Lowly privates like us or maybe even Old Stonewall Jackson himself," Vance mused. "Papers say he likes lemons. Don't see any lying around."

"Horse shit means officers," Mitchell came back and grinned.

"Don't it always in more ways than one?" Bloss added and chuckled. Then he noticed a yellowish paper package lying in the tall grass between Mitchell and Vance. "What's that between you and Vance, Mitchell?"

"An envelope," Mitchell said. "Looks like trash to me."

"Hand it to me," Bloss said, rolling over and scattering a couple of honeybees.

Vance picked up the package. As he passed it to him over Mitchell's chest, out fell three small cigars. Mitchell grabbed them, fondled one between his thumb and forefinger and sniffed it. "Good Southern tobacco. This is mine, since they all got dumped on me. Vance, you get this, and Sergeant, you can have the third. Anyone got a match?"

"Hold on there a minute," Bloss said, opening the envelope and pulling out a letter. "Let me read this first." He quickly perused it and could not believe what he was holding. "Listen to this!" he said,

22

hardly able to contain himself. More of the company gathered around. Bloss cleared his throat and began, "HEADQUARTERS, ARMY OF NORTHERN VIRGINIA, September 9th, 1862, Special Order, No. 191."

"Sweet Jesus!" Welsh blurted.

"Shut up," Campbell snapped. "I want to hear it. All of it."

Bloss continued, "Three. The army will resume its march tomorrow, taking the Hagerstown road. General Jackson's command will form the advance, and after passing Middletown, with such portions as he may select, take the route toward Sharpsburg, cross the Potomac at the most convenient point, and by Friday night take possession of the Baltimore and Ohio Railroad, capture such of the enemy as may be at Martinsburg, and intercept such as may attempt to escape from Harpers Ferry."

"Hey, that was four days ago. Today is Saturday," Welsh said.

"Will you just shut up?" Campbell snarled.

"All of you, just shut up and let me finish," Bloss said, glaring at the men around him. Then he continued. "Four. General Longstreet's command will pursue the same road as far as Boonsboro, where it will halt with the reserve, supply, and baggage trains of the army." "Five. General McLaws, with his own division and that of General R. H. Anderson, will follow General Longstreet; on reaching Middletown he will take the route to Harpers Ferry, and by Friday morning possess himself of the Maryland Heights and endeavor to capture the enemy at Harpers Ferry and vicinity."

"Six. General Walker, with his division, after accomplishing the object in which he is now engaged, will cross the Potomac at Cheek's Ford, ascend its right bank to Lovettsville, take possession of Loudoun Heights, if practicable, by Friday morning, Keye's Ford on his left, and the road between the end of the mountain and the Potomac on his right. He will, as far as practicable, cooperate with General McLaws and General Jackson in intercepting the retreat of the enemy."

"Seven. General D. H. Hill's division will form the rear guard of the army, pursuing the road taken by the main body. The reserve artillery, ordnance, and supply trains, etc., will precede General Hill."

"Eight. General Stuart will detach a squadron of cavalry to accompany the commands of Generals Longstreet, Jackson, and McLaws, and, with the main body of cavalry, cover the route of the army and bring up all stragglers that may have been left behind."

"Nine. The commands of Generals Jackson, McLaws, and Walker, after accomplishing the objectives for which they have been detached, will join the main body of the army at Boonsboro or Hagerstown."

"Ten. Each regiment of the march will habitually carry its axes in the regimental ordinance-wagons, for use of the men at their encampments, to procure wood, etc."

"By command of General R. E. Lee, R. H. Chilton, Assistant Adjutant-General." Bloss fell silent, still dumbfounded.

"Shit," Vance blurted. "Marching orders … the whole damn plan for the next four days from that time for all of Lee's army!"

"You got that damn straight. If genuine, this paper in my hand and the information on it is extremely important, even if none of this happened yet," Bloss returned.

"Anyone got a match? I'd still like to …" Mitchell started.

"Put the cigars back in the envelope," Bloss ordered.

"Hey, not fair," Mitchell protested.

"War's unfair. … So's life. Do it," Bloss insisted with a glare.

"You ain't fun at all, Sergeant," Mitchell said but complied.

"That order has to be real," Vance said to get everyone back on track.

"If so, why was it just lying around here?" Welsh demanded.

"Can't answer that for sure. Maybe a courier dropped it. Doesn't really matter the why of it. What matters is the importance of it. I'm taking it to Captain Kop. Corporal Mitchell, you take over

24

while I'm gone." He adjusted the straps on his knapsack and picked up his musket.

"Hey, boys, we're all gonna be heroes. This order might end this whole damn war, if we get the drop on the Rebs," Vance said and grinned.

Bloss headed off down the line with the package in hand to find his company commander, as the men talked excitedly among themselves over the joy of the information they discovered. He spotted the young captain only a hundred yards away. He jogged over. This could not wait a moment longer. "Captain Kop, sir. Got something here of great importance. You might want to have a look."

Kop turned to him as he saluted. Kop returned the gesture. "What's all the excitement, Sergeant Bloss?"

"This, sir. Looks like orders from Lee." He handed Kop the letter and kept the three cigars in the envelope.

Kop read the order. His eyes widened with disbelief. "Where in God's name did you get this?"

"Found it just lying on the ground where we halted. We all thought it was trash at first."

"We've got to get it to Colonel Colgrove immediately." He handed it back. "Come with me. He can't be far. This might even earn you a promotion."

"I'd have to decline any promotion. I got enough paperwork just being a sergeant, sir."

Bloss stuffed the order back in the envelope with the three cigars. On foot, they headed further down the skirmish line. They had jogged about a half mile when they spotted a familiar gray-bearded officer on a bay horse and headed for him.

"Colonel Colgrove," Kop yelled as soon as they were in voice range. "You've got to see this, sir."

The Colonel turned his horse toward them as they approached.

"Captain." They saluted, panting from the exertion of walking. Bloss handed the package to the colonel, quite pleased with himself.

"Sir, Sergeant Bloss here seems to have found orders from General Lee. Marching orders to all his generals," Kop said upon catching his breath. "Figured if they're genuine, they might be valuable, though a bit outdated."

The colonel read the orders quickly. "Sergeant, you have just done your country a major service without firing a shot. I'll see you are commended for this."

Bloss felt the warmth of full-blown self-satisfaction surge through him and savored it. Such moments were rare. This day was turning out quite good after all.

The sound of approaching horses drew their attention to the left. It was Brigadier General Nathan Kimball and his staff, probably inspecting the skirmish line, Bloss figured. The officers rode over to join their little group. Colonel Colgrove saluted General Kimball and said, "My compliments to the general."

"Colonel. What's all the excitement about?"

"Sir, you may want to read this. Seems Sergeant Bloss here has come across an order from General Lee." Colgrove handed the general the order.

Bloss and Kop stood waiting while the general read. A smile could just be seen through his dark beard. "Colonel, I'd say your sergeant has just done us a great service turning this in. It looks genuine. Could change the course of this damned war. Why, it could all be over in a week, gentlemen. I'm giving you permission to bypass my headquarters and have a courier take it directly to Brigadier General Starkey Williams, the acting XII Corps commander. He'll get it directly to General McClellan."

Their work done, Bloss headed back to the company with Kop after being dismissed. He would have liked to have brought the three cigars back, but in all the excitement he could not remember if Colgrove or Kimball had taken them. *No matter*. His place might just be secure in history. If nothing else, it would be a worthy story to tell his grandchildren … if he survived.

To See the Elephant

"Jeremy Franklin, you get back here!" Amanda yelled, running after her younger brother. "Mama will skin you alive when she gets home."

Jeremy ran toward the gate of his Aunt Catharine's picket fence in front of the white farmhouse, past a patch of side yard that had been plowed up by a cannon ball. "I'm thirteen today and can do what I want!" he yelled over his shoulder.

He was tired of hiding out in the root cellar under the house. The ordeal started when a Confederate artillery battery came thundering past the barn, and a mounted officer rode over and told Aunt Catharine to get her family to a safe place. That was two days ago. A furious battle had raged yesterday on both sides of Antietam Creek only a couple of miles down the road toward Sharpsburg. Jeremy had spent all of yesterday listening to it, cowering in the dark with his mother, Amanda, and Aunt Catharine. He had not been as frightened as the women. He wanted to see the two great armies before they marched away. Maybe even find his Uncle Richard, a captain in the Stonewall Brigade, or his father with Stuart's cavalry.

He never expected the Rebel army would invade Maryland while they were all visiting from Shepherdstown just across the Potomac. The battle had delayed their return trip. Now was his last chance to break away and have a look while his mother and Aunt Catharine were checking on an elderly neighbor down the lane who meandered past the farm to the Hagerstown Pike.

Amanda had been left to watch him. He didn't need watching. He vaulted the fence as he caught sight of Amanda, skirts flying, running around the side of the house. She was eighteen and wore her raven hair in sausage curls, her eyes brown as a doe's and presently hard with anger. She had a new beau, Tim Smith, also with Stuart's cavalry. Jeremy figured she thought that made her his boss. It turned his stomach to think any man might be interested in her.

"Jeremy, you come back here now!"

"No, and you can't make me," he taunted and tripped through a puddle in the lane, his shoes kicking up clots of mud. His trousers got spattered and his feet wet, but he did not care. When he looked over his shoulder again, Amanda was at the gate.

"I'm going to tell Mama you went to find Papa and Uncle Richard. You will not go unpunished." She shook her fist at him.

He laughed and kept running down the lane. He ran for another hundred yards and then slowed to a walk, venturing to look back over his shoulder. Amanda was headed back to the house. He figured she'd give up her screaming once he was far enough away.

Mama and Aunt Catharine had told them both to stay in the house. There was no telling what manner of men that might come by, Mama had warned. He did not care. He had nothing to fear. He was finally free of Amanda. Free to find the armies. He planned to join Stuart's cavalry when he was old enough, if the war lasted that long.

Since the newspapers published the first report of the firing on Fort Sumter with the black-and-white engravings of tumbling walls and exploding shells, he was lured by the adventure of it all. He remembered how jealous he felt when Papa joined the cavalry and left with their bay gelding, Scout. Under the bed at home, he had a cardboard box filled with all the newspaper articles he had collected on the various battles, along with Papa's letters. When not doing chores, he spent hours rereading the letters, looking at the engravings of straight battle lines, rearing horses, puffs of smoke. He thought it all so glorious and noble to fight for a new country. He could not understand why Mama did not want to look at the newspaper any more.

A light afternoon breeze teased the tall grass in the field immediately to his left. He noticed areas had been trampled down by the passing of men, saw wheel ruts he assumed were from the Confederate artillery battery that had passed through his aunt's property. There was more plowed-up earth.

He broke off a seedhead stalk of grass in passing and stuck the end in his mouth, chewing it slowly, thoughtfully. Maybe he'd come back later and dig up the cannon ball for a souvenir and the one back at the house, too. He squinted at the road ahead, searching for more signs of any army, fearing they may have all pulled out. He had no idea if the battle that raged yesterday was over or who now occupied the area.

At a few distant cracks of muskets, he dived behind a big walnut tree on the side of the lane. His heart raced. Maybe they were the skirmishers like he had seen in the newspapers. But whose? Or maybe they were pickets taking potshots at one another.

He pressed his back against the rough bark, waiting, listening, anticipating. Nothing. He grew bored, disappointed. There wasn't going to be a battle with flags waving and little puffs of smoke he could sit and watch. He left the tree and continued his walk down the lane.

He passed woods and a field gone fallow and weed-choked. Above the woods he spotted five turkey vultures and numerous crows circling in an overcast sky. A mockingbird sang from the green shadows at the edge of the woods. It was just like any other autumn afternoon he had ever known except for the more than usual number of vultures and crows in the sky.

The breeze shifted. With it came the acrid scents of smoke and powder and something that reminded him of the half-rotted winter-killed deer he found in the woods last spring. *I must be close.* A sudden chill ran through him. He did not know why. He stared at the woods and fields, studying the shadows and thick brush searching, hoping.

Distant voices called above the creak of wagon wheels beyond a stand of woods out toward Dunker Church. He could not understand the words. The talk was garbled by distance. The lane went up a hill where it met with the Hagerstown Pike. He planned to head toward Dunker Church. Most of the battle noise had come from that direction yesterday. Troops might still be there.

When he crested the hill at Hagerstown Pike, he froze. A few yards away, across the pike amid the rocks and trampled-down grass by a rail fence was a row of dead men in ragged Confederate uniforms. Some looked as if they had just been thrown to land there from a great height. They were blackened and swollen from the sun, staring with vacant white eyes. Scattered around them were blankets, tin cups, canteens, and muskets. A rotten stench hung over it all. Flies buzzed everywhere. Suddenly unable to move, all he could do was stare.

He had never seen a dead body before out in a field. They did not look to be in a peaceful sleep like his grandfather had in his coffin at the viewing in April. A thought pushed through the shock. He realized the newspaper engravings lied, and he felt betrayed. They never showed this. The battlefields had all been a remote reality, like a funeral next door. Now the real mangled bloody truth was staring him in the face. He suddenly felt bile rise in his throat and fought to swallow it back down.

"Come to see the elephant, farm boy? Found it ain't a pretty sight, haven't you?" A gruff voice behind him made him jump.

He turned to find two Confederate soldiers carrying a third in a blanket slung between them. One was taller and had a cut on his cheek, the other shorter with broad shoulders. The one in the blanket was thin and pallid. All three were ragged and dirty, their faces smeared with black powder. They could not be much older than his sister.

"This ain't a circus," he said, confused by the comment, trying not to throw up in front of them and embarrass himself. He backed a few steps up the lane.

The shorter man chuckled derisively. "No, it ain't."

"See the elephant means see the war, boy," the tall one continued.

The sick feeling passed. "I get it. But I also thought I might find my pa or my uncle Richard. My pa's with Stuart, and my uncle's with Jackson."

His pride in them had not waned despite the carnage around him. All sorts of conflicting emotions began to churn within.

The soldiers headed toward Jeremy. He could see the man in the blanket was unconscious. A red stain covered a bloody bandage around his left thigh.

"Do tell," the tall one said. "Just hope they ain't in Jim's shape here. If they ain't, they'll be with their units. We just come back for Jim."

"Yanks and you, farm boy, will have to bury them fellers," the short soldier said, nodding toward the fence.

They passed him heading toward Sharpsburg. He started to follow them. "Who won?" he asked.

"Does it matter?" came the shorter soldier's bitter remark. The man in the blanket groaned. They stopped and put him down on the side of the road. Jeremy stepped closer.

"Jim, you want some water?" the tall soldier said, reaching for a canteen slung over his shoulder.

"Could use some," Jim said weakly. "God, this hurts."

"The ambulance should be by soon. Just saw it on the hill a few minutes back while you were out cold," the shorter soldier said. The tall soldier handed Jim the canteen, then turned to Jeremy and frowned. "Why don't you just git on home? Your mama's probably wondering where you got to."

32

"Can't," he said, frowning, resenting being treated like a child. "My home is on a farm outside of Shepherdstown. I'm visiting my aunt."

"Well, then, get back to your aunt's house. This ain't no place for you. Yankees might come at us again. Got enough worries now with Jim. Don't want you on my conscience, too," the tall soldier said.

The approaching horse-drawn ambulance bumping and jostling down the pike toward them stopped further conversation. Jeremy found himself totally ignored as the two men lifted their friend and headed down the road toward the ambulance.

He started to follow but decided against it and just stood on the side of the road staring. He watched them put Jim in the ambulance. Then he turned away and started to walk toward Sharpsburg, suddenly not wanting to go near the ambulance. He didn't want Jim's companions to think he was being nosy.

He got about ten yards, heard the ambulance creak. A man moaned; another delirious man screamed out nonsense. *They are haunting me*. He dared not look back at the ambulance or across the road at the corpses. He started to run toward Sharpsburg.

"Can't take looking too close at that elephant, can you, farm boy?" The short soldier's voice reached him, taunting and critical.

It made him run harder. He had no answer, no scathing comment to hurl back. Only knew he did not care to hear any more and resented the two soldiers. But the farther he ran, the worse the carnage around the road became. The dead men of both sides, along with a few horses, were scattered in every direction he looked. The horror of it all numbed his senses. His eyes stared to fill with tears. What if Pa or Uncle Richard are out there shot and nobody comes to help? Please, God, no! His breath rasped in his throat. The foul air he was sucking in made him feel sick again, but he had to keep running. He had to get away. He had to …

33

"Jeremy! Jeremy, is that you?" his father's voice called from his right.

He stopped and turned, lungs feeling about to burst. There, galloping across a plowed field on Scout was his pa. He looked so different, bearded now and covered with dust in a grimy gray shell jacket with corporal's stripes, a saber rattling against his left leg as he rode. He ran to meet his father, a flood of relief coursing through him.

"What in God's name are you doing out here?" Pa said, pulling Scout to a stop.

Panting, Jeremy felt as if his knees would give out. He had to grab Scout's breast strap to keep standing. "I … Ma and Amanda are at Aunt Catharine's. The battle. We couldn't get home."

"Is everyone all right?"

He caught his breath, legs steadier. "Yes, Pa. But a cannon ball plowed up the ground on the side of the house."

"Well, you shouldn't be out here. I'll take you back. Got special permission to check on Aunt Catharine." He held out his hand. "Take my hand and I'll pull you up behind the saddle. Scout can carry us both."

He nodded and reached up his hand. His pa hoisted him to Scout's back as if he weighed no more than a chicken. He grabbed his father tightly around the middle and leaned his cheek against his sun-warmed back. He felt safe now. Joy, pain, grief, and relief tumbled in a confused lump in his chest. "Oh, Pa, I didn't know it was like this."

"War ain't pretty, Jeremy. It scars the people and the land in more ways than I care to think about."

His pa put Scout into a trot. They headed back down the pike toward the ambulance. Jeremy did not want to go that way, but they did not have a choice. The ambulance was now between them and the lane that lead to Aunt Catharine's. He did not have to look, but he did, unable to keep his eyes away.

The horse pulling the ambulance plodded along slowly, lifting its head and pricking its ears at Scout. The driver glanced up at Pa.

"You better head on into town. Word is Lee wants to be on the way to Shepherdstown by evening," his pa called to the driver.

The man nodded his understanding. As they passed, he noticed blood dripping from the back of the ambulance. The tall soldier driving the ambulance and his companion, a shorter soldier walking along behind it, seemed not to notice the blood. They looked up. The tall one saluted lazily.

"Corporal, we retreating?" the tall one asked, stopping.

Pa reined in Scout. "Nothing more can be done in Maryland. Went scouting this morning. Found fresh Federal divisions coming in and reported it. Our army's in a bad way right now. Took heavy losses. Not enough men left to fend off another major attack."

"Shit," the shorter man said.

"You boys better get back to your unit," he said and got Scout walking again.

"Your boy?" the tall one asked.

"Yes."

"Glad he found you. Leastways, this battle had one happy ending," the tall soldier called after them.

Pa put Scout into a trot again. Jeremy's grudge against the two soldiers melted. He found himself praying they'd be all right. Then he closed his eyes to the carnage around him and concentrated on the movement of Scout beneath him, knowing each hoof fall brought him that much closer to Aunt Catharine's farm and the secure shelter of his family.

Amazon

She had survived. Kathleen O'Riley could not believe her good fortune. She had survived and fooled them all. She, a skinny seventeen-year-old girl with nothing to look forward to but a life of washing floors and doing laundry for rich people, had fooled the arrogant bigots who would keep her down.

In the eyes of society, she was just a woman ... and worse. She was Irish. Home for her and her twin brother, Charles, had been two rooms in a lower Manhattan Bowery tenement since their parents fled Ireland in 1851. That is, until her restless, rebellious spirit had been given a cause to fight for ... freedom; freedom for herself and her people. Charles, though less volatile in nature, shared her ideals.

The man responsible for her revelation had been a kindred spirit—Major-General Thomas Francis Meagher. Once a brilliant orator in the Young Ireland Movement, an organization in his native land that fought for Ireland's independence from Great Britain, the dashing and eloquent Meagher was now leader of the Irish Brigade in the Army of the Potomac. A true son of Erin, his silver-tongued recruiting speeches impressed upon all, "Every blow you strike in the cause of Union is aimed at the allies of England, the enemy of your land and race."

Any fool on the streets of the Bowery was keenly aware that England had close ties to the Confederacy. This fight for their adopted country would be the dress rehearsal for going back and freeing Ireland from the British tyranny. Her zeal led her to do the unthinkable.

Now she was standing in line in a blue Federal army uniform under a heavy light blue overcoat identical to those Charles wore.

36

Her brother stood next to her, the frigid December wind blowing around them in the war-ravaged town of Fredericksburg. She had signed on as Sean and did not let the fear of discovery daunt her determination for her cause. After all, despite society trying to break her, she felt she was following in the footsteps of the famous Celtic warrior queen Boadicea, who led her tribe against Roman invaders. She would not be thwarted from that path. Since she had cut her auburn hair short to sign up with Charles over seven months ago, it was harder than ever to tell them apart. Being small breasted, it was easy to keep herself bound up tight with the remnants of her old bed linen, and she had managed to hide her monthlies. Her voice was slightly deeper than most girls her age and a lot louder, as Charles and her father often reminded her.

The patriotically blind doctor performing the physicals had done little more than look at everyone's throat, teeth, and eyes and ask how they felt in order to pass as many new recruits as possible. Besides, she shared her tent with her brother at the training camp. No one wanted to tempt fate and break up the twins, and he continued to be her tentmate in the field. The only regret she had was her parents thought she had run off with a local boy. A belief Charles did nothing to correct.

The thunder of artillery and crash of muskets of a major assault brought her back to the present. She looked around at their regiment. Under a noon-day-turned-to-dusk by the smoke and storm of battle beyond the town waited the 69th New York, one of five regiments in the depleted Irish Brigade, now down to twelve hundred men, the amount that normally made up a regiment. Beyond them among piles of brick from shattered buildings and all along the street were the bodies of Union and Confederate soldiers, a reminder of the grim house-to-house fighting that had secured the town for their crossing of the Rappahannock River on the pontoon bridge.

She was suddenly aware of the cold passing right through her shoes and two pairs of socks, and stamped her feet to bring back the feeling. "Wish we would get moving," she groused to no one in particular. "I can't stand all this waiting. My feet feel like blocks of ice."

Charles looked up at her from adjusting a sprig of boxwood on his forage cap held in his hand. "Don't know why you're in such a bloody rush to die."

"My, aren't we in a good mood this noontime," she shot back, letting anger chase away the sudden chill of a growing fear he might be right. Luck could only last so long, and they had both already been in their share of bloody battles, starting with the second day's fighting at Fair Oaks during the June Peninsula Campaign. They only missed the bloodbath at the Sunken Road at Antietam in September because they had both been debilitated by intestinal problems at the time and declared unfit for duty.

"We are all going to die. You know that. We aren't going in with our green battle flags, since they all got shot to pieces and the new ones haven't arrived. A bad omen, it is. These sprigs of boxwood Meagher told us to put on our caps are a pretty poor substitute if you ask me," Charles continued, putting on his cap.

"No one's askin' you, O'Riley," Patrick O'Connor piped up next to him, big, dark-haired, and the eternal optimist. "The 28th Massachusetts over there has theirs still, and it looks like they're takin' the center post. We won't be without a green banner goin' in."

"Green or no, open your eyes, man. We'll be goin' up that hill," Harry Donovan said behind them, a beanpole of a man. "Up that hill against artillery and dug-in infantry. The officers must be mad. Stark ravin' mad. It'll be a bloody turkey shoot, us bein' the turkeys."

She took a long hard look at the rise of ground outside the town. The assaults of French's division and Hancock's leading brigade had been torn to pieces. The dead and wounded, along with hundreds of dazed survivors, lay in crooked lines on the bullet-swept snowy slope. The stone wall above erupted in a sheet of flame. Still more

38

men dropped. She had to look away, outrage knotting cold in her stomach.

Charles suddenly gripped her upper right arm, pulled her close, and whispered, "You don't have to stay here. Faint. Act like you're sick and go to the rear. No use in our parents losin' both of us."

She glared at him. "What about the others? They'll think I'm a coward. I ain't a coward. I can't leave them or you."

"You ain't a man. You do not have to do this. You shouldn't do this. You should be home. Find a husband."

"What, and live in poverty no more'n a white slave to the rich? What's the matter with you, Charlie? You know I can handle myself in combat. You never acted like this before. You were all for my comin' along."

"This ain't combat. It's suicide."

The men were suddenly moving for the edge of town. She pulled away from her brother, her heart hammering in her chest. He was suddenly beside her again.

"For the love of God, don't do this, Sean!"

The thunder of artillery half drowned his words. She pretended she could not understand as she hurried away to follow the others across a narrow bridge over a millrace, her musket bumping on her shoulder as she jogged. She saw bodies floating in the water, looked away. The outrage became a hate that crushed the panic that tried to rise. Shellfire savaged the congested column, but they got through. Charles caught up to her as the brigade formed its battle line. She glanced over at him and swore she saw tears in his eyes.

All around her, soldiers in the regiment were unslinging packs and blankets to unencumber themselves for the coming assault. She shrugged off her pack and dropped it at her feet but kept her canteen and haversack.

"Please," her brother said as they waited for the inevitable.

Her heart was stone. She would not, could not give in. She was not a slave to any man. Nor were the Irish. And if it took her blood to prove it, so be it. The Irish Brigade was known for fighting gallantly against long odds … and taking heavy losses. They were her brothers-in-arms, and she would never let them down. When the time came, she'd be shooting at British troops with the same élan. Suddenly, she spotted General Meagher limping along in front of their battle line. His handsome face was smoke-stained, his dark eyes sharp.

He waved his sword and shouted, "Irish Brigade, advance! Forward, double-quick, guide center, march!"

The line surged forward, muskets at a right shoulder shift. She went with them, hearing a bullet whine past her ear. She did not even blink at it. At Fair Oaks she learned you never hear the one that kills you.

Amidst the deafening roar of artillery, her voice joined the rest in cheering a hoarse *Faugh-a-Ballagh* (Clear the Way)! She noticed another brigade come with them as support and was aware of Charles still at her elbow. They passed over piles of the fallen and into the smoke and flame that engulfed the hellish heights. She was put in mind of the stories of purgatory Father Sheen had terrified her with when she was a small child. At the blast of artillery, gaps were opened through their formation, but the ranks closed up and pressed on.

As they reached the first fence, the Rebel infantry sheltered behind the stone wall opened fire. She was going over the top rail when Harry Donovan fell hard against her, knocking her down, too, in a crash and tangle of muskets. She ended up flat on the frozen ground with him across her back. She lay there stunned a moment, then called out in the din, "Harry. Harry, you all right?"

She twisted half around and shoved his shoulder. No response.

"Harry?"

Suddenly, Charles was beside her. He bent over and pushed Harry off her. "He's dead. Half his head's gone. If you have any sense, you'll lay there yourself, Kate," Charles pleaded.

He threw himself over her as a shell exploded only yards away. Covered with bits of frozen earth and spatters of blood, their faces close to each other, they lay there a moment, panting clouds of breath. She pushed against the earth with her elbows to get up. "Charlie, you hurt?"

"No. You?"

"No."

"Good. I'm not letting you up."

"Oh, yes you are, or I'll make you. And you know I can."

She balled her hands into fists, twisted around, swung with her right, and managed to punch him in the side of the head. It surprised her as much as him.

"Bloody hell!" Glaring at her, he grabbed both her fists and pinned her more solidly to the frozen earth. "Look at the heights, Kate. They ain't gonna make it. Not a chicken could get to that wall alive."

The steam of his breath blew in her face. She twisted her neck to glance up the hill. Only partly visible in the drifting battle smoke, the brigade was going over a second fence, leaving behind more dead and dying in its wake. It looked like almost half the brigade was gone.

"Let me up! Damn your hide!" she yelled, still watching as the charge sputtered out before the stone wall in tangled heaps of dying men and writhing wounded.

The survivors began blazing away, kneeling or lying prone in the human wreckage. Tears of frustration and disgrace started to run from her eyes down her half-frozen cheeks. The futility of it all was finally registering, dampening the fire in her heart. The men who could started to make their way to the rear and rallied around their tattered unit colors. Others stayed, pinned down by the hellish rain of lead.

She looked back at Charles above her. Anger flared again. He had no right to hold her back. He had no right to make her a deserter.

41

That was more than just a brigade. Those were their friends out there. Didn't he understand? Didn't he care?

She brought her knee up hard and sharp into his groin. He cried out and fell to the side. She grabbed the shoulder strap of her musket and dragged it over, picking it up as she stood.

As she turned toward the flaming hill, something hit her in the ribs on her right side with such force that it spun her around. She hit the ground hard, biting her lip.

"Sean! Kate!" she heard Charles yell. He crawled to her side.

When she took a breath, the searing pain in her side cut it short. She had the metallic salty-sweet taste of blood in her mouth. Her worst nightmare now had her in its grip. Panic crept in. "My ribs. I'm …"

"Sh-h-h-h. Don't talk. Don't move," Charles said as he lay beside her, fumbling to open her overcoat and the sack coat and shirt beneath it.

Another shell exploded near them, and he threw his arms over her face. When the debris stopped falling, he thrust his hand into her clothing. She felt his probing fingers over her binding and screamed when he touched the open wound. A rib shifted, and she was aware of a warm wetness.

"I'm so sorry, Kate," he cried, his lips close to her ear.

She took a painful, ragged breath, turned to look at him, and saw tears in his eyes. "How bad?"

"Near as I can tell, it's shallow. Rib's broke. Bullet must have grazed you. But you need a doctor's care. You know what that means. Secret's out."

She closed her eyes half-wishing the injury was fatal. Now she'd be going back to her parents' tenement as nothing more than a scullery maid. There would be even more insults. Woman in a man's world. Unnatural. How dare she? Nothing but a whore who will roast in hell.

42

"I can't go to a hospital. Ribs heal easy. Just need a bandage." Patrick O'Connor was suddenly crawling up to them, rifle still in hand.

"You hit?"

"I'm fine. Sean's been grazed. Got a busted rib and the wind knocked out of him." Charles lied for her.

She could see resignation in his eyes. She could have kissed him for that, and a pang of guilt hit because of having kneed him. It was her foul temper, she reasoned, brought on by the miserable circumstances of her life.

"Well, don't stand unless you want to meet Saint Peter. I'll stay with you, and come nightfall we can get Sean to a surgeon. Can't do a bloody thing on this hill. From what I seen, we lost half the regiment. Saw our Colonel Nugent taken off the field … and General Meagher. We're in a terrible fix."

She said nothing. She was fighting hard to stay conscious. She opened her eyes, focusing on the two men.

Patrick reached out to pat her shoulder. "Hang on, Sean. You'll be all right, me boy."

Charles pulled a bandanna from his coat pocket. "Sean, I'm going to put this on the wound. Don't move."

She saw him reach in, felt the sting of the bandanna on the raw edge of the gash, and stifled a cry.

"You need some water?" Patrick called over the din as he crawled closer to her, reaching for his canteen.

"Thanks, Patrick. Maybe later," she said with great effort. "Don't think I could keep it down."

Patrick nodded and left the canteen hanging against his hip.

"We got at least another three hours of layin' on this frigid ground before the sun goes down," Charles said.

"Don't know about you, but me balls feel like they're kissing me kidneys," Patrick said and grinned at her. "Tryin' for a little humor here, but it's the truth."

43

"Maybe we ought to start crawling back now like some of them other boys. Long as we stay low, we should be all right," Charles said as a shell screamed past over them.

"I agree. Better idea," Patrick said. "No sense in waitin' any longer than we have to, with Sean needin' a surgeon. One place is as safe as the next in this slaughter pen."

She was beginning to feel worse and nodded.

"Leave the muskets. We'll need our hands free. Can always pick up another one later. God knows there'll be plenty to choose from," Charles said grimly.

With Charles and Patrick on either side of her, they grabbed her cartridge belt and began slowly crawling and dragging her under the fence past other wounded men, back toward the bridge over the millrace, which might as well be a million miles away. The firing slackened around them somewhat, shifting to concentrate on the next line of suicidal attackers pushing up the hill. They would have to go through the battle line. There was no way around.

Though Charles and Patrick made every effort to avoid bumps in the ground, each time they pulled her after them, the coats bunched, and a sharp stab of pain shot through her side. She slipped into merciful darkness, only to be awakened by the explosion of a shell close by. When her vision cleared, she saw the next battle line moving past them in the long shadows of a setting sun, closing a gap torn by a shell that hit only yards from them. The millrace and bridge were just a few paces away. She felt detached, as if she were watching all from someplace far away. It made her feel so helpless.

Patrick reached out and grabbed the pants leg of a corporal passing close. "It's suicide up there! Turn back, for the love of God!"

The corporal pulled free, raising the butt of his musket as if about to strike, but continued past instead.

"Bloody fool!" Patrick shouted after him. At the bridge he stood up. "Come on, Charlie. It'll be easier on foot to get him across."

44

He got up, and they hoisted her between them, throwing her arms over their shoulders. The rib shifted and she groaned. The darkness came again.

When she came to, she found herself being carried in a blanket slung between them and was aware of a confused mob of men and horses milling about on both sides. Some of the houses were burning. She knew she was closer to town now. The old panic returned.

"Wait," she called out hoarsely.

The two men stopped and gently set her down. Troops passed and barely gave them a second look. They were faceless in the crowd of walking wounded moving to the rear.

"What?" Charles said, squatting next to her.

"I don't want to see a surgeon." She struggled to sit. "Just bind up my rib."

"Don't talk nonsense," Charles said, putting a hand on her shoulder and gently pushing her down.

Patrick kneeled beside her. "Brave lad, just stay put. We don't have far to go."

He and Charles picked her up in the blanket sling again. She could see the roof and second floor of a shell-battered brick house. A dazed man limped past and glanced at her.

"No," she protested. Then she made a decision she feared she'd regret, but perhaps there was just the smallest chance she would gain an ally. After all, they had been through hell together. "Charlie, tell him … tell him the truth."

"Are you crazy?" Charles blurted.

"Huh?" Patrick blinked, confused. "The only truth I see is we better get movin'. This ain't the place for discussions. Looks like a field hospital might be in that house. Let's see, Charlie."

"Wait. Please, Charlie," she said, reaching out and grabbing his hand.

45

"Wait," Charles said and Patrick stopped. "Let's get off this road and over to that carriage house."

"If you say so," Patrick said. "Must be important to cause such a fuss when we should be gettin' Sean here to a surgeon."

They passed a broken fence and entered the shelter of a bullet-scarred carriage house. They were not alone. Many wounded had gathered there, some on old straw brought in for bedding. All had wounds of various severity bound up in bloody rags. Some writhed and moaned, while others stared with vacant eyes at the dark rafters. One sergeant standing by the shattered door with his arm in a makeshift sling looked them over and pointed to the back of the dark carriage house. "Still plenty of room back there. Go on and make him comfortable. Hospital steward should be back any moment."

Patrick and Charles carried her all the way to a quiet corner in the back of the building next to a box stall and put her down gently. Charles got her half seated and put a grain sack behind her shoulders, wrapping her in the blanket.

"All right, what is this great truth you have to be tellin' me?" Patrick asked as he squatted next to Charles.

"Patrick, you got to promise to take it without a fuss ... an' keep your mouth shut about it," she said, pain numbed some by the cold.

"Bloody hell! What is it that can't be talked about? The suspense is killin' me," Patrick said, leaning toward her.

Charles sighed. "Sean is my sister. Her real name's Kathleen."

Patrick's eyes went wide, and his jaw dropped open. "What? Am I hearin' this right? Sean is your sister, you say?"

"You heard right," Charles said. "That's why he's ... she's refusing to see a surgeon."

Patrick flopped backward to sit on his butt. "Holy Mother of God!"

"Sh-h-h-h! Please, not so loud," she said, trying to lie still to keep the pain at bay.

46

"You ... him ... brother and sister?" Patrick rambled on, dumbfounded. "All this time with us ... men? How'd you...? And fighting like the Devil himself. No. Really?"

"Yes," Charles said.

Patrick covered his face in his hands. "This ain't right. It just ain't."

"What's done is done," Charles said. "And you got to give her credit for stayin' on with us, Patrick. She's my sister, and she's proven to me a woman is stronger than we give 'em credit for. And whoever said a woman can't fight must know nothin' of history. There's the Amazons ... an' ... an' even our own people tell of Nemhain, who cursed Cú Chulainn's warriors and made a hundred of them drop dead on the spot."

"And the warrior Queen Boadicea," she added. Patrick sat there staring at them, shaking his head.

"Well, in the light of things now, you'll be goin' home. You ain't no warrior queen. This ain't no place for a lady."

"I ain't no fancy Fifth Avenue lady with Irish servants," she snapped, leaning forward. She suddenly grimaced from the pain and sat back. "I ain't going back there to be some rich bitch's charwoman. I'd rather walk into those Rebel guns on that bloody hill." She met Patrick's amazed stare with an icy glare.

"You got spirit, I'll give you that," Patrick said. "I think ..."

"Don't you dare patronize me," she snarled and felt her face flush.

"Will you just hush and let me have me say?" Patrick drew closer to her and Charles. "God knows I'm not the kind of fellow who tells others how to live. But there's a part of me that believes your place is at home with your lovin' parents. You might even find a nice fellow to settle down with ..."

"I'll not ..." she started.

"Damn it! Let me finish!" Patrick snapped.

She fell quiet and glared at him.

47

"I know the tenements ain't nothin' much above squalor. Me own mother is stooped like an old woman from scrubbin' floors for the upper class. I share your dream for a better world. Understand? So as much as it pains me to see a fine young … woman … as yourself continue to face the ordeals of combat and camp, you made a choice and have the courage to stick by your ideals and your friends. I ain't goin' to step in your way. I'll keep your secret. Will probably burn in hell for it. But I'm figurin' I'll be burnin' in hell anyway. Besides, I might even be able to help. Maybe we'll fix things so's you don't need no surgeon."

A smile spread on her face.

"How?" Charles said.

"You got to get a better look at the wound, and that calls for a lamp. I'll check the house next to this place to see if I can find one. If that wound don't need much beyond a few stitches and a tight bandage, I got a needle and thread in me coat pocket and can do the sewin' if you don't have the stomach for it, Kathleen bein' your sister an all." He grinned.

"And if it is more serious?" she asked, not wanting to face the answer.

"Then you'll have to see a surgeon and go home," Patrick said, standing. "Charlie, you stay here. Watch for that hospital steward, and stay back here so he don't nose around. I'll be right back." Patrick left quickly.

She closed her eyes and settled back against the grain sack, praying to God Almighty she'd not be so quick to judge if He'd get her through this without discovery. Charles stayed close, watching for the hospital steward. It was not a long wait.

A portly man in a corporal's uniform with wire rim glasses and a green arm band denoting his medical duty appeared at the entrance of the carriage house and started checking on the wounded men out front. Her heart pounded in growing panic as she watched him make his way slowly toward her and Charles.

48

"Let me do all the talking. I'm goin' to do my best to keep him from examining you," Charles said.

She nodded and watched him move to stand between her and the steward as he approached.

"What have we here?" the corporal asked pleasantly, then frowned at Charles.

"My brother. Not serious. Bullet grazed his ribs. One's broke," Charles said.

The steward looked around Charles, then gently pushed past. "I need a closer look, son, to evaluate …"

She struggled to sit up. "I'm just a little sore and got a scratch. I ain't gutshot or nothin' like that. My brother is worse 'n an old mother hen. Could've stayed an' kept shootin' if he and a friend didn't drag me off to this wretched place."

The steward stopped and stared at her over his glasses. "Feisty little Mick, ain't you? You can wait, then, until the more serious cases are seen to." He turned to Charles. "Is that all right with you?" The tone was sarcastic.

"Yes, fine," Charles said, backing toward her.

"Then I suggest you get back to your unit. There's some of them gathering down the street by a green flag. He'll be fine where he is." The steward turned and walked away, carefully stepping over and around the wounded scattered on the floor of the carriage house.

She lay back, getting an instant reminding stab of pain that she may be a victim of wishful thinking. But so far, so good. Her secret was safe.

Charles breathed a sigh. "If that weren't a crock of blarney, I don't know what was." He sat down next to her. "You want some water?"

She nodded, and he handed her his canteen.

Patrick came back with a lit lamp in one hand and a pillowcase with something in it in the other. "Here we go. I'll hold it. You look," Patrick said, kneeling close to her.

49

She unbuttoned the overcoat, and Charles helped her peel it back. She opened her sack coat and pulled up her shirt, noting the patch of blood on both her shirt and the piece of bedsheet she used to bind her small breasts. The bandanna Charles had stuffed over the wound was soaked. The sight of it made her feel faint. She felt the color drain from her face. She looked away and noticed Patrick was averting his eyes. Charles gently pulled the bandanna away and undid the binding.

"This might hurt," he said, an understatement.

She stifled a cry as he poked around the wound. She dared to look. It was an ugly, open gash about half an inch wide that followed her broken rib for about six inches around her side. The area around it was turning black and blue.

"I'd say you were lucky. It looks nasty, but it's all on the surface. Could use a stitch or two," Charles said. "But then, I ain't a surgeon." He looked up at Patrick. "You can get out your sewing kit now."

She saw Patrick turn to look, and she instinctively pulled her shirt down enough to cover her exposed breast.

"Must say, Kathleen, you're turnin' such a lovely shade of blue. Charlie, hold the lamp and keep one eye out for that damn hospital steward." Patrick forced a smile, handed the lantern to her brother, dug his hand in his coat, and pulled out a spool of black thread with a needle stuck in it. "Must say when Mum sent this, I never thought I'd be usin' it to sew somebody's hide. And that somebody bein' my friend's sister, who I thought was his brother, silly me."

She stifled a laugh. Patrick was such a joy to be around. She watched him thread the needle and bite the end of the thread. "Looks like it'll take about ten or twenty stitches if I make 'em small. You want something to bite on?" he said, looking her right in the eye.

There was still that twinkle of humor. She nodded. To cry out would attract too much attention, even with all the moaning around her. She grabbed the edge of her coat and bit down.

50

"Charlie, try not to drop the bloody lamp." He took the first stitch.

She bit down harder on the coat until her jaw cramped, and she found herself counting each searing poke. When he was finally finished, he poured some water from the canteen over the stiches, and she jumped from the icy feel of it. She pulled the coat out of her mouth and dared to look, surprised how neat the stitching was … and then fainted.

She awakened to someone splashing a few drops of cold water on her face. She was all dressed and bundled up in her overcoat again. Her ribs were bound tight with some kind of support. When her head cleared and her eyes focused, she found herself sitting between Patrick and her brother in the dark.

"If you're feeling a little stiff, its 'cause you're wearin' part of a corset. Found one in the house. Cut it down some. Don't need all the frilly lace. Figured the whale's ribs could provide the support yours can't for a while. You're wearin' a fresh sheet as a bandage, too," Patrick said, capping his canteen. "I got some extra in me haversack for later."

"Come on, let's get you on your feet." Charles took her gently by her upper arm as he started to stand. Patrick took her other arm. She stood with them, feeling a little wobbly and very grateful.

"I owe you, Patrick," she said.

He just smiled and nodded. "Think we better get out of here and try to find what's left of the regiment. You feel good enough to take a little walk?"

"I'll make it," she said, feeling sore.

"Good for you, Sean, me boy. Can't keep a good man down." Patrick grinned.

"And you'll not be breathin' a word about Kathleen?" Charles asked.

"Kathleen? Who's Kathleen?" Patrick said. "Your girl back home?"

They left the carriage house and walked into the night to become just three more soldiers among the milling troops on the debris-laden streets of Fredericksburg.

The Last Battle

Darkness was closing in. In the twilight woods and tangled thickets, officers were losing contact with their men. Colston and Rodes's units were becoming scrambled and confused as they pursued the fleeing Federals in the growing darkness. In front a sudden burst of shelling was answered. Trees were shattered by aimless blasts of metal. The enemy had to be kept running. They could be crushed now.

General "Stonewall" Jackson would not give them a chance to reorganize. He never did like the nickname "Stonewall". It was too pretentious, and he was a humble man before God. It was the men who stood that day at Manassas. He only gave the order.

"Press on! Press on!" he shouted from the back of Little Sorrel. "Keep moving toward United States Ford! They must not escape over the river!"

For the last two hours, he had been riding forward to urge his men on, his staff hard pressed to keep up. Each time wild cries of victory echoed through the murky forest, he looked skyward and gave thanks to the Lord. One of his young staff officers rode up, and he recognized him. It was the younger brother of his wife, Anna, Lieutenant Joseph Morrison.

"General Jackson, they are running too fast for us. We can't keep up with them," Morrison said in jest.

He turned a stern gaze on the youth and replied, "They never run too fast for me, sir."

The attack sputtered to a halt in the darkness. An unearthly lull settled over the battlefield. What rising moonlight penetrated the thick tangle of woods illuminated drifting smoke that hung low to the ground, giving the wilderness a dream-like quality.

He reined in Little Sorrel, the staff slowly gathering around him. He looked past them and saw a red glow low to the ground south of the turnpike. Another. Then, yet another. He wanted to ride on to the confused tangle of Colston and Rodes's troops to tell them to keep moving on the enemy, but he felt the deadweight of dismay. He could not see anything in front of him and knew they could not either. Attack in the dark made no sense in a tangled place like this.

"My, God, that glow. The woods are on fire," another staff officer said, riding up.

The acrid smell of powder and smoke permeated the air. The wounded called for help. Pleading. Crying. Distant screams told of those caught in the fires. The dream was a nightmare.

His will was steel. No time to mourn. Men lived or died by God's will. He grew impatient. The moon brightened. Light cut through the darkness. He could see the shapes of the staff around him—the glint off horses' bits and metal sword scabbards, the trees, and wide path of a road in the milky gloom. God was showing the way. He rode over to one of his staff officers.

"Tell A. P. Hill to move forward, relieve Rodes's troops, and prepare for a night attack."

Hill, a Mexican War veteran, handsome and volatile, he trusted above all of his division commanders. The officer rode away into the moon shadows. He knew the Federal troops were out there, maybe not too far away. He checked his watch. It was 9 p.m. He could waste no more time.

He rode ahead along a trail with several of his staff officers to scout the enemy lines near the Plank Road. In the darkness, broken only by small pools of moonlight, they moved slowly over unfamiliar ground, through thickets and tangles of briars as they worked their way toward the enemy lines. They turned down a small road. Straining to hear, he stopped the horse.

54

There was the clear sound of digging, the cracks of axes and crash of trees being felled for enemy breastworks. Orders were shouted, echoing through the woods. They were closer than he thought. But sounds always carry further at night. He motioned to the staff, and they began moving down the trail. The deafening blast of a cannon, one of Hill's by location, sent a pointless blind shot toward the Federal lines. Several bright flashes answered. Tree limbs shattered and fell from above. They kept moving through the dark. A burst of musket fire came from their front. An answering volley exploded in the woods to their right.

A hand touched his shoulder to the anxious whisper of Lieutenant Morrison, "Sir, this is no place for you. We are well beyond our lines."

He held up his hand. The little group stopped. He understood now that his attack would have to wait for morning. "You are correct, Lieutenant. Let us return to the road."

He turned Little Sorrel away, and his staff followed him, all working their way quickly along the trail. There was movement in the brush ahead.

"Halt! Who goes thar?" a voice demanded.

"It's Yankee cavalry! Fire!" came a sharp command.

A volley lit up the woods, tearing through their group. Officers fell. Horses screamed, plunged, and went down. How could this be?

"Cease firing!" Lieutenant Morrison shouted at the pickets in the darkness. "You are firing into your own men!"

"Who gave that order? It's a lie," came a strong, hard derisive answer from an officer obviously used to deceits. "Pour it into them, boys!"

Another volley raked them. Jackson spun Little Sorrel around and tried to reach the shelter of trees on the other side of the trail. He felt the sharp blow of a bullet strike his right hand, and two more punched his left arm hard. No pain yet. Only shock, disbelief, and the wet warmth of blood.

Little Sorrel squealed, terrified, and bolted into the woods toward the enemy lines. Jackson lurched in the saddle, trying to get a better grip on the reins. He had to bring the horse under control. Branches hit him, almost knocking him from the saddle. He made another grab for the reins with his wounded hand, caught them, and turned the horse onto the Plank Road.

Something shifted in his left arm. The searing pain hit, unrelenting. He felt himself slipping from the saddle. There was more shouting. Horsemen were galloping toward them along the trail.

Hill's familiar voice yelled toward his lines, "Cease fire! These are our men! Cease fire!"

An aide was suddenly beside him, sobbing. Then another officer rushed over in the darkness. They got him off the horse and carried him to the side of the road. An aide started ripping the sleeve of his wounded arm. Each move sent waves of sharp pain up to his shoulder.

Hill rode up, the expression on his bearded face looking more solemn than usual in the moonlight. "Oh, God. General, is the wound painful?"

"Very painful," he replied. Turning to look in the pale light, he saw a dark stain covering his left shoulder. "I fear my arm is broken."

A surgeon rode up and inspected his wounds. "The bleeding has slowed. Moving him could start the flow again," he warned.

"You have to get him out of here. A Federal counterattack can start any moment," Hill responded gruffly.

They carefully got him to his feet, but when he tried to walk, he was quickly exhausted. A litter was brought up by four bearers. Just as he lay down, Federal artillery opened up. Hellish thunder. Too close. Shells hissed through the thickets, and shrapnel swept the road as they rushed along it. One of the litter bearers was hit in both arms. As he was lowered to the ground, another panicked and ran for cover in the dark woods. Jackson struggled to rise. He needed shelter from the storm of iron.

Captain James Smith of his staff was suddenly bending over him, restraining him, shielding him with his own body. "Sir, you must lie still. It will cost you your life if you rise."

Grapeshot struck sparks on the flinty rocks in the moonlit road around them. He noticed their own artillery moving along the road to the front. Orders were shouted over the thunderous din. Horses and men were swept from their feet, screaming, broken, bleeding. When the firing veered away, Smith got him to his feet, and they staggered into the woods. The litter was brought over. He was helped on. So weak. Cannot ... must not give in. Smith and three others raised the litter to their shoulders and started for the rear again through the dark, tangled woods and drifting smoke. Suddenly, one tripped over a root. He was thrown to the ground and landed on his shattered arm. The pain was too much. A groan escaped his lips for the first time. They quickly got him back on the litter. He felt distant, his mind moving far away.

Brigadier General William D. Pender of A. P. Hill's division rode up. "Sir, the situation is confused. The lines here are so broken that I fear we will have to fall back."

The shock from loss of blood and pain did not stop the words from rousing him. "You must hold your ground, General Pender," he growled weakly. "You must hold your ground, sir."

Smith finally found an ambulance. "This is General Jackson. Get him to the closest field hospital," he heard Smith tell the driver as he was put in the back.

His mind drifting, he endured a bumpy ride to a field hospital at Wilderness Tavern. There Dr. Hunter McGuire, his old friend and corps medical director, found him. He was aware of faces and movement. McGuire examined his arm, his eyes grim.

"Thomas, I am afraid it might be necessary to amputate your left arm. The bone is shattered, and the artery in your upper arm is severed."

"Yes, certainly," he answered quickly, thinking the Lord's will be done. "Do for me whatever you think best."

Hospital stewards moved closer to the head of his bed.

"We at least have some chloroform to make this easier for you," McGuire said.

He glared at his old friend and shook his head.

McGuire drew closer. "This is not a test of courage, General. You need not endure pain to please God."

He smiled. McGuire knew him too well. Nodded. Closed his eyes. A brief prayer. "I must obey the doctor. Forgive me and guide his hands. May Your will be done." Then he felt the soft cotton on his face and breathed in the sharp chemical smell. He took a long deep breath. His mind began to spin and pull farther away. With the chloroform came the blessed darkness and a relief from the terrible pain.

He lost track of time. Nights and days blended and became fuzzy. He could remember, barely, talking with Captain Smith and General Pendleton, that he had been moved to the Chandler house below Fredericksburg at Guiney's Station, and had seen McGuire's calm, gentle face. And then there was the needle, and his mind would fog. Dreams would come; the flames, the roar of the guns and crackle of muskets, the shouts, horses screaming, men falling. Then reality would wash in like a tide.

His breathing was short and painful. A clock ticked in the distance. He heard quiet, distant, familiar voices.

"He is healing well, but there is a problem," Dr. McGuire said through the fog. "I'm afraid he has pneumonia."

A death sentence. He knew this.

"Please, Doctor. May I see him?" It was dear Anna, praise God.

"Certainly, but remember the medication makes him drift. He may not recognize you or the baby. And he is very weak. Lieutenant Morrison, would you please escort Mrs. Jackson in?"

He forced his eyes open. The room was so white. There were people. He struggled to focus. Morrison came in with dear Anna and little Julia. She stared down at him and suddenly could not look any longer. She dropped down, holding the happy gurgling baby close, and laid her head on his chest. Behind her, Morrison left the room. Jackson wanted to wrap her and little Julia in his arms as he had always done, but he could not move because of the weakness.

"*Mi esposita,*" he said. It was his pet name for her. He felt her soft sobs and a tear slide down his own cheek to pool, then soak into the pillow. He closed his eyes and began to drift away again.

When he came back, they were gone. He could not sleep. The pain every breath caused would not let him. McGuire was back with his needle. It would not be long now.

He was aware of the soft, white glow of sunshine. He could smell Anna and the baby nearby. He tried to focus, but they were gone.

The sun was glowing through the trees and sparkled on a river. From somewhere on the other side came the distant, low thunder of artillery. He looked around to find he was alone. The army had gone on without him.

The light grew brighter on the other side. There were soldiers near him; a small group mounted on horses under tall oaks. One officer held the reins of a riderless horse. It was for him, he knew. A gentle voice sounded. "It is time. He is waiting."

"Let us cross over the river and rest under the shade of the trees."

The Great Mudbug War

The June sun illuminated fresh green leaves that sent dappled cool shadows spilling along the quiet banks of the sluggish Rappahannock River. The plop of a jumping fish sent ripples of light in concentric circles, the liquid sound breaking the stillness with all the power of the shattering of glass.

Hardly making a sound himself, James Anderson padded through the brush barefoot in his ragged gray and butternut uniform, a slouch hat pulled low on his head with the crown punched to a round dome. This was his sixteenth summer and the worst one yet. In his right hand he carried both a musket and a fishing pole. The musket was loaded at half cock, with a percussion cap in place on the nipple of the lock, a brutal reminder of his present world. The fishing pole, just the opposite, stirred cherished memories of a peaceful past of idle summer hours at a favorite fishing hole on his aunt's plantation. His left hand brushed branches out of the way. As he walked, he glanced at the sluggish river once in a while, ever alert for those people on the other side.

Those people, blue bellies, Yankees—it was all the same to him—were the enemy. A faceless and soulless blue army, defeated at Chancellorsville and licking its wounds on the other side of the river. Only a few weeks past, the battle had been bloody work, he recalled. A few of his friends had fallen. What was supposed to be so glorious in defense of land and a way of life had left holes in his heart.

He pushed the dark thoughts from his mind. The river was calling. To hell with the war and guard duty. The day was too good to waste on war and killing. There were fish to catch.

At a more open spot on the bank, where a large flat boulder leaned into the green water, he paused. He studied the river. By the look of the slow current, the water was moving over a deep hole in the riverbed. In the shallows were reeds and a few water lilies. It was a perfect spot to fish.

Cautiously, he crept out on the rock and set his musket down within easy reach. He put his fishing pole next to it. He dug in the haversack slung over his shoulder for the peach can full of worms. In no time he had the hook baited with a plump night crawler, tossed it into the river, and settled down on the sun-warmed rock.

As tempting as the river was, calling his mind to wander, he did not allow it to lull him into a false sense of security. A part of him was fully aware of his exposed position. So, he decided to divide his attention between watching the cork float bobbing gently on the water and the far bank, where brush and trees could hide the approach of *those people*.

Only a thrush called from the green shadows over there. An early cicada buzzed its song above him, and all was right in the world. He let his gaze wander back to the cork float. It bobbed and dipped under the water. He pulled up on his pole, feeling the weight of the fish as the pole bent almost double. He stood up and backed up the rock to the bank, hauling hard. A huge bass broke the surface, fighting wildly until a last deft yank on the pole landed the glistening fish on the rock. James quickly pounced and grabbed the line, dragging the fish over into the grass. He got it off the hook and laid the gasping bass safely in the grass. He smiled broadly. Then he rebaited the hook and settled to await the next catch.

Jeremiah Spooner, in a well-worn blue uniform, was approaching his riverbank post with all the stealth of a hunter, rifle loaded and ready. Splashing had alerted him that he was not alone. He could not believe the brazenness of the Rebel soldier he glimpsed through the brush just sitting across the river, fishing. He was in no mood for such an affront. His regiment, the 20th Maine Volunteer

Infantry, had nothing but hard luck from the day it arrived in the theater of war in September. They had been held in reserve at Antietam. Then in December they were trapped on Marye's Heights at Fredericksburg for thirty-six freezing hours. January was almost as bad when they got mired in mud trying to surprise Lee in his winter quarters. And worst of all, they were held in quarantine because a bad batch of smallpox vaccine had caused eighty-four cases of the disease that kept them out of Chancellorsville, which turned out to be yet another Union fiasco. At this point, he and many of his friends doubted if they would ever do their part in ending the rebellion. They had yet to be in a real stand-up fight. As far as he was concerned, he was ready to do his part right now.

He kept his aim on the Rebel and took another step past a drooping branch for a clearer view of his target. His foot crushed a stick hidden under tall grass, and the loud crack it made might as well have been a rifle shot. His heart leaped and he felt stupid. The Rebel instantly dropped his pole, grabbed his rifle, and dived for the cover of the brush next to the rock before he could get off a shot. Jeremiah pulled back to the cover of a tree trunk.

"Who goes there?" James demanded, his heart pounding in his chest. He saw movement in the brush and demanded louder, "I said, who goes there?"

"You stay right where you are, Johnny Reb," Jeremiah yelled in his most commanding voice, angry at himself for being so damn careless where he put his feet. He leaned against the tree to steady his aim.

James could just about see the shadow of his enemy in the brush next to an oak and shifted his aim a little. He only needed slightly more of a target for a clear shot. That is, if his enemy really wanted a fight. "I ain't movin' from this post, Billy Yank. 'Sides, the fishin's too good."

"Well, I certainly ain't moving from my post," Jeremiah yelled back, feeling his arm begin to cramp from the weight of the musket.

"No one's askin' you to, but you make a mighty easy target so close." James thought that a good bluff.

"So do you." Jeremiah was getting impatient fast. He was not about to lose this war of nerves. *No one could out-stubborn a Maine man,* he thought. Leastwise a sorry-ass Reb.

Bird song and the gurgle of the river flowing past filled their sudden silence for what seemed an eternity.

James suddenly noticed the cork float bob violently. *Damn, this fool is ruining my fishing.* "Don't know about you, but my arms are gettin' a might tired. And a fish is playing with my bait."

Jeremiah's thoughts of blasting this Rebel out of existence suddenly starting to fade. He seemed to like fishing. It was unexpected common ground. His own family's business was fishing, digging oysters, and running a lobster trap line. He had even brought a hand line from home. This whole hostile stance was suddenly starting to look a bit foolish. He wondered. "Want to call a truce?"

James had a glimmer of hope his whole day would not be ruined. "Sounds like a good idea to me, Billy Yank. You come out first."

"How do I know I can trust you?" Jeremiah shot back

"I ain't in the habit of lyin', and you ain't no challenge to shoot. Be murder, not war, like in a battle," James returned.

Someone had to make a move. The words were somewhat encouraging. Jeremiah threw caution aside and stepped out from cover, still aiming at the splash of gray he could see between the leaves across the way. "I ain't putting my gun down till you do the same."

James smiled to himself and stood up, still aiming and calling out. "Fair enough. Let's do it together."

They both put their muskets down, watching each other suspiciously.

"Is the fishing really that good here?" Jeremiah was seriously wondering at this point.

"Yep." James bent over and slowly held up the large bass he had hauled out moments before the disturbance. He looked at his enemy across the river, still unsure.

It was a fine fish. Jeremiah could not help smiling. "Mind if I join you? We can keep an eye on each other while we fish and not get into trouble with our officers."

James took it as a sign things were all right, at least for now. He put down the fish. "Fine with me. I don't have no claim on the Rappahannock." He picked up his pole and settled back on the rock. "But you'd best stay on your side. Don't want to start no battle over a damn fishin' hole. Personally, I'm gettin' mighty sick of this whole damn war."

Somehow, Jeremiah found he was not that surprised at the Reb's words. "To tell you the truth, so am I. What's your name, Johnny Reb?" He watched his ragged enemy as he settled on a nearby log half in the river and took the hand line out of his greasy haversack.

"James Anderson. What's yours, Billy Yank?" the Reb returned, still eyeing him suspiciously … or maybe it was his imagination.

He nudged over a rock with his toe and quickly snatched up a fat worm, baited the hook, and tossed it in the river. "Jeremiah Spooner. Where you from in Rebeldom?"

James allowed himself to relax more. "Was born in New Orleans. Was twelve when my pa died, and I moved with my ma and four sisters to her parent's plantation outside of Birmingham. Where you from?"

"Rockland, Maine. Family owns a fishing boat," Jeremiah said proudly. "I work it with my pa and two brothers. Dig oysters and trap lobsters, too. Or at least I did until I got all fired up and joined the 20th Maine last summer. Who you with?"

64

"The 15th Alabama," James answered, not really wanting their talk to go back to the war. He decided to head it off. "You must be good at fishin', then, it being your family business and all."

"Pretty fair when conditions are right."

"You like it?"

Jeremiah felt he should not hold back. "It's damn hard and sometimes dangerous work. Not pleasurable like tossing a line in a stream and sitting back to enjoy the day like we're doing."

"Fishing like this is the most pleasurable thing a man can do." James found himself smiling broadly.

"Amen to that, James. Take this any day over marching and fighting."

They both fell silent a moment to watch their cork bobber and lightly tug on the line as if of one mind and body.

"Oysters," James said, suddenly voicing his thoughts. "They're a delicacy for rich people. My Aunt Betty featured them at one of her fancy balls. Shipped them in from Mobile on ice. I can't see how people can eat them things. Must be like eating snot. How in blue blazes do you catch them? Dig 'em up or something?"

"You don't catch them. You use an oyster rake and wade in during low tide and just rake 'em up and put 'em in a basket."

James nodded and smiled. "That makes sense."

Jeremiah felt a fish play with the bait. Then there was a light steady pull. "Think I got one," he said and pulled hard to set the hook.

In a small explosion of white water, a brown trout broke the surface, trying to throw the hook.

"Whoo-eee! Looks like you got one of fair size," James called, glad the fishing luck was good for the other side.

The trout dived to continue the fight, but Jeremiah was quicker. He hauled it in hand over hand and held up the dripping, flapping fish. "Trout, I reckon. Or what passes for trout in these parts." He quickly removed the hook, put the fish on the bank, grabbed a grub

65

from under the overturned rock, rebaited and tossed the line in the river. If his luck held, he knew he could feed the whole company something better than salt pork and hardtack and maybe keep from getting chewed out by Lieutenant Birch.

"There are good-sized catfish here, too," James said, breaking into his thoughts. "But they're a bit puny compared to what I pulled out of the Mississippi when I was six years old. Hooked into one off the levee that was almost as big as I was. My pa had to help me pull it in."

"Go on! You're pullin' my leg."

"No, Jer. It's the God's honest truth. There're channel cats that come upriver from the Gulf. Some grow to be damn near the size of a man. You must have caught some big fish in the Atlantic Ocean."

Jeremiah always liked fish stories. He decided at that moment he'd give James something to think about. "My pa hooked into a swordfish once. Took all of us to haul it in. Weighed near five hundred pounds. Dangerous fish. Fights back something fierce. Has a big bill like a sword."

"Ha! Now who's tellin' fish stories? A fish with a sword on its nose. Next, you'll be telling me about harpooning sea monsters."

A fish hit his bait before he could add to the teasing. "Whoa, got another."

He pulled in a modest-sized trout, got it off the hook, and quickly rebaited.

"It's the God's honest truth, James. You ever been to sea, way beyond the sight of land, out to the blue water and rolling swells?" Just talking about it brought a wave of nostalgia. He could just about smell the ocean.

"I reckon not. And I ain't likely to either. River's enough water for me. Can get pretty choppy when there's a storm."

"Afraid of the sea?"

"What?" James could not believe he was being challenged.

"Are you afraid to go to sea?"

"No, I just ain't got no inclination to leave land."

"Well, there's a lot of big fish out there." Jeremiah found himself smiling. "Some even bigger than that swordfish my pa caught. A whale shark for one. That's bigger than our fishing sloop."

A crazy notion hit James so hard in the funny bone he laughed. "Sure you ain't from Texas and got transplanted?"

"Texas!" Jeremiah burst out as if it was an insult.

"Yep, Texas. They got the biggest of everything … or so I've heard them brag. Biggest state, biggest cattle ranches, biggest you name it."

Jeremiah smiled. "Sounds like those fellows are all mouth, like some fish."

James's infectious laughter danced again across the river. "You got that damn straight. Speakin' of big mouths … we ought to shut ours a spell. Think we're scarin' off the fish."

"You might be right, James. You might be right."

They fell silent, letting the river sounds and bird song soak away all bloodstained thoughts of war until only the present tranquility was their reality.

———○———

Jeremiah sat on the log, content for the time being, his line attached to a pole this time. He had brought a sizable catch back to camp. It had been enough for his company and officer's mess. The reprimands had melted with the presence of real food. This morning his friend, Ezra, had even given him a bean can full of night crawlers before he left for guard duty. Yet as he watched the bobber, he knew he could not be complacent. He watched the opposite river bank, his musket in easy reach loaded and ready. There was no guarantee that the guard across the way would be the amiable James Anderson today.

At the sound of crackling brush, he dropped the pole, grabbed his musket, and settled behind the log with the barrel balanced against it, aiming across the river. There was silence for three hard pounding heartbeats. He felt a drop of sweat slide down his chest under his grimy shirt and the heavy wool sack coat. The cracking and light pop of brush sounded again.

"Jer, is that you at the post cross river?" came James's familiar drawl.

Jeremiah sighed with relief. "Yep, just me. You gave me a bit of a fright." He got up, put his musket to one side, and took up his pole as James pushed through the brush, his musket and pole over his shoulder in a casual manner.

James down put his musket, settled on his rock, pulled a can of worms from his haversack, baited his hook and tossed it in the river. "Everything go all right for you last night in Yankee land?"

"Got a bit chewed out by Lieutenant Birch for fishing while on guard duty. That man's a real pain in the brass, if you know what I mean," Jeremiah returned, thinking of the red-faced officer who nearly had apoplexy at the sight of him carrying a line heavy with seven bass and five trout back to camp.

James grinned. "Yep. We got a few pains in the brass over here, too."

"But the company sure appreciated the fresh fish. The company cook made sort of a fish chowder of my catch. Managed to add some potatoes, onions, and carrots to it that we got from the cold cellar of an obliging farmer. Much better than salt pork and hardtack. Got orders for another catch … when I'm not watching for you and your crowd, who according to the top brass might be crossing at any point and anytime. They've all been real nervous since Chancellorsville."

James laughed. "Officers are always nervous about one thing or another. Sounds like your diet ain't much better than ours, but at least you got food."

"Now, maybe, as bad as it is, but when we get to marching, half the time we get only what rations we draw beforehand. Often as not it has tenants already munching on it. Still, the officers have to warn some of the boys to make it last."

"Know what you mean, Jer. But now we got us a good source of fish. Nothin' better 'n a fried catfish or trout."

"That's for damn sure. Miss my ma's cod cakes something fierce."

"Had cod once. Was dried and salted. Even reconstituted it didn't taste too great. Like dirty socks with an aftertaste of fish."

They both laughed. James's pole suddenly jerked. He quickly fought a large bass into submission and hauled it in. "What I miss in the way of fish is my ma's catfish fritters and hush puppies," James said, a little breathless from the struggle. "She stopped makin' them when we moved to my aunt's plantation. My Aunt Betty would not let her cook. She had a darkie do all the cookin' in her house. Made a real lady of my ma. Never lifted a hand again to do any housework, let alone cook. Well, maybe now that your Mr. Lincoln freed the slaves, my ma will have to cook again. I know I look forward to those catfish fritters and hush puppies when I go home."

The sudden thought of home fell heavy on Jeremiah's heart. "Lord knows when either of us will be getting home the way things are. Damn the men that started this whole war anyway."

"Was the politicians that done it, according to my Uncle Matt," James said with assurance. "They started it, and we end up fighting and dying. Of course, that John Brown had a hand in it. You ain't one of them abolitionists, are you?"

"Good Lord, no," Jeremiah said, pausing only long enough for a deep thought to surface. "But I do believe in freedom for all men."

"Well, it don't make no difference to me." James felt a sudden anger that seemingly came out of nowhere. "I just want you fellows out of the South and to be left alone. Don't care for politics or officers or …"

The sharp words shocked Jeremiah into the deadly reality they were living. "Let's not get ourselves all worked up. We just got to be friends."

The calming words and the soothing gurgle of the water around the rock cooled James's anger. "Yep, you're right. Neither of us has anything personal against the other. We are kindred spirits in liking to fish. Why, you could be my neighbor back home. It's going to be an awful thing if we run into each other on the battlefield someplace."

"No need to get all depressing now. No need to …" Jeremiah's words were cut off by the sudden sensation of his bait being played with and dragged in a light but steady pull. He quickly yanked up his line to find a large crawfish clinging tenaciously to what was left of a worm. "What the …?"

James looked over, saw the crawfish and laughed. "Got yourself a mudbug, did you?"

"Got myself a damned bait-stealing crawfish. What in blue blazes did you call it?"

"A mudbug. That's what we call them in Louisiana. Ain't you got any mudbugs up there in Maine?"

Frowning and careful not to get nipped, Jeremiah pulled the crawfish off his mangled bait and tossed it into the river. A funny thought hit with the plop of the crawfish in the water. Grinning, he looked at James across the way. "Sure, we got some big mudbugs. The biggest mudbugs in the whole damn country. We call them lobsters."

"There you go with the oversized seafood again." Jeremiah rebaited his hook with a fat worm and tossed it in the river.

"Honest, James. These crawfish are poor, puny things compared to their seagoing cousins. Why, the biggest one we ever got in our traps was nearly fifty pounds. Caught it two months before I joined the army. Was the talk of Rockland for a month. Almost took my thumb right off when I was helping my brother get it out of the trap." He held his thumb up and wiggled it at James across the river. "It still hurts when it rains."

"A fifty-pound mudbug? Come on, Jer. I was born at night, but not last night," James said, sure this was a real fish story.

"Well, if it weren't last night, you must have spent your life under a rock if you never heard of or seen a lobster."

"I ain't been under no rock. I seen a picture of one in a book once. And we get a different kind from the Gulf. Just can't believe a seagoing mudbug could get that big."

"You ain't seen a Maine mudbug … er, lobster … up close and personal."

"No, I must admit that. But I do know Louisiana mudbugs are real good eating. Could eat a whole bucket full right now with some gumbo." The thought made his stomach growl with anticipation.

"Don't need a whole bucket of lobster to get satisfied. Our average is about two to five pounds."

"God Almighty, Jer. You're worse than the Texans with your fish stories."

"It ain't a story. It's the truth. It's the God's honest truth. We had a fifty-pound lobster. I still got the scar to prove it. And the normal ones *are* two to five pounds."

James shook his head and smiled. "I just don't know about you, Jer. Seems to me maybe you Maine fellers are trying to outdo the Texans in tellin' tall stories. Fifty-pound mudbugs …"

A fish hit his bait, derailing his thought. He pulled up a small bass, quickly rebaited the hook and tossed it into the river.

Jeremiah started laughing hysterically.

"What in tarnation has gotten into you, Jer?" He could not imagine what was so funny about tossing a baited hook into a river or a fifty-pound lobster, if there was such a thing.

Jeremiah laughed even harder at the thought that had hatched in his mind. He laughed so hard he could hardly breathe.

"You're beginning to worry me, boy," James called to him.

Tears in his eyes, Jeremiah finally got some control. This was a thought that had to be shared. "I just … I just thought …"

"Oh, you can really think? Ain't used up all your air laughing like a hyena?" James's words started the giggles boiling over to laughter again.

Jeremiah forced a deep breath to get the words out before he busted a gut. "I just came up with the answer."

James was confused. "Answer to what?"

"The real reason for this war."

"You mind sharing it with this ignorant Reb?" James grinned.

"Mudbug envy."

"What?"

"The Texans could not stand it that Maine had the biggest mudbugs, so they got South Carolina to fire on Fort Sumter."

That was too much to bear. They both broke into hysterical laughter, the unbounded mirth echoing up and down the river.

James got control first. "I'm so glad I met you, Jer. Now you've finally set this whole war thing straight for me, letting me know it's the damn Texans' fault. And let me know you Yankees have a good sense of humor to boot. I hope I never see you after this. No offense."

His chest hurting, Jeremiah finally got control. "No offense taken. I feel the same about you."

"Too bad we two ain't in control of things. We could end it all right here and now, and I could go home to my catfish fritters and you to your lobsters."

"You got that damn straight. Tell them all to go fishing with one another. They might learn something of the real world."

With a grin so big he felt it would crack his face, James said, "Can just see the headlines now. Two Fishermen End the Great Mudbug War."

They both broke into laughter again.

It did not matter that there was a twelve-inch-thick tree trunk between him and the Rebels. Jeremiah never felt more like running in his life.

For almost two hours his regiment had stubbornly held the rocky side of Little Round Top at the far left end of the Union line against repeated Rebel attempts to crush them. He had fired his musket until it was almost too hot to handle. From what he could see of their position through the battle smoke hanging like fog, it now looked as if half the regiment was down, those killed or wounded mingled with the Rebel dead and wounded, among the blood-slick rocks and underbrush. Even the trees bore witness to the brutal fighting, scarred by bullets up to the height of six feet, the thinner saplings cut down. The left wing of the regiment was bent back against the right. The worst area of casualties was the center immediately to his right. They had been hit by three-way crossfire. Only three men of the color company were still standing, with the tattered flag there among their fallen comrades. He had seen his commanding officer, Colonel Chamberlain, not far from the colors only moments before the last attack that had broken through their line in vicious hand-to-hand fighting. He missed the colonel's cool confidence-building presence, fearing he may have gone down in the last attack they had only barely managed to repulse.

Below their position the battle smoke and brush masked much of what was going on, but by the rattling of equipment and shouting, the enemy was reforming for another attack. Jeremiah knew in his heart they could not take another attack like the last one. The last half hour had been filled with desperate calls for ammunition. The officers had told them to take it from the cartridge boxes of the dead and wounded, but even that was running out now.

He saw Sergeant Clark, only twenty-one, with a grim look on his smoke-stained face heading toward him along their ragged line.

73

Growing more frantic by the second, Jeremiah had to voice his dire plight. "Sergeant Clark, I just fired off my last round."

Clark paused to look at him. "You and most of the rest of the boys."

The increased crack of muskets and boom of artillery from the other side of the hill made him suddenly feel queasy. The enemy had probably broken their brigade line and was going to slaughter them all. "We ain't going to be able to take another attack like the last one."

"Pray the colonel comes up with a plan." Clark patted him on the shoulder.

He watched Clark head toward the center, but the sergeant only got one step and froze as Colonel Chamberlain limped into view, using his sword as a cane, just beyond through the battle smoke. He still looked to be the dignified college professor with his erect stance and full, backswept mustache despite the smoke stains across his face and dusty uniform. The colonel stepped to the right of the colors, raised his sword and yelled, "Bayonet!"

There was so much noise coming from the other side of the hill, the order was heard only by those close to him. Jeremiah looked in disbelief back at Chamberlain but then pulled the bayonet from its scabbard and fixed it on the muzzle of his musket, as Clark did the same next to him. Others down the line saw them and fixed bayonets as officers passed on the order.

Chamberlain yelled, "Forward!" And the order was almost immediately lost in the loud and fierce cheer from many throats glad for the release of the awful tension and the turn of a defensive fight into an offensive one as they started their charge down the hill, dodging bodies and rocks.

Jeremiah moved forward at a half crouch, bayonet ready and yelling, as Clark did the same next to him. The wild charge down the hill took the Rebels by surprise. Many ran. Others threw down their muskets and surrendered. Jeremiah made his way down the hill, passing bushes, jumping logs, meeting no resistance. He was conscious of men passing him and sporadic shots. Then as he slowed to dodge a tree near a bush, a hand suddenly reached up to grab his pants leg, almost tripping him.

It was an enemy soldier. Startled, he stopped and raised his musket to defend himself with the bayonet. A weak but familiar voice reached him through the fog of battle that covered his mind. "Jer ... Jer, it's me. Jer, remember the mudbug?"

Jeremiah froze, the bayonet inches from his enemy's chest. He looked at the pale, smoke-stained face and suddenly remembered who it was. Instantly, he dropped to his knees, putting his musket aside.

"James, you ... hurt?" He tentatively touched James's shoulder.

James reached out a bloody hand to grip his shoulder, his face contorted in pain. "It ain't good, Jer. Took a hit in front of my hip. Oh, God ... I never wanted it to come to this."

"Easy." He turned to check the wound, finding the edge of James's tattered coat and trousers stained in the dark red blood of a deep wound. He could not look further. He knew his friend was gutshot.

"Got this far ... couldn't go no further," James struggled, his voice almost a croak. "Don't want to die in a prison, Jer. Been bleedin' like a stuck pig. ... Innards feel like they're on fire."

Jeremiah felt so helpless, but he had to do something. He had to try. "Got to be honest with you, James. It looks bad. I've got to get you to a field hospital."

He started to stand, but James grabbed his sleeve, stopping him.

"Your field hospital? I'm a prisoner for sure." He did not want to die in a federal prison.

"No, your field hospital." That answer was no good. James shook his head. "Then you'll be a prisoner. ... No, Jer. Just let me go like you did that ol' mudbug last month."

"I can't. You need help," Jeremiah insisted.

James frowned and struggled to sit but failed, frightened and amazed at how weak he was now. He felt an anger rise at the cussed hardheadedness of his Yankee friend. "I said ... I didn't want to see you again ... remember?"

"Yeah, I remember."

He grabbed Jeremiah's arm with both hands and shook it with what little strength he had left. "Well, I meant it. I know you mean to be kind ... but I meant it ... now git!"

"But ..." Jeremiah could not just give up, though he could see James was fading fast. "No one should die alone," he found himself suddenly thinking.

"Damn it ... don't go hardheaded on me like a damn mudbug." He wondered if it was getting darker or his vision was starting to fade. He felt a peacefulness creep over him in spite of his angry words.

"I can't do it, James ... and you better not talk so loud. My friends might be back any moment. You got to let me help. Neither of us started this mess. I want to stop it. I want to get you to a doctor. You need ..."

James saw the world slip away to brightness like light playing on the surface of water. He suddenly went limp, letting go of his friend's arm.

"James! James!" Jeremiah grabbed James's hand. He reached out to feel for a pulse on his neck. It was useless. He was refusing to see the reality around him. Only James mattered. And the way the light played on the river. If he looked hard, he could see it again. A gut-wrenching remorse filled him. "Damn it, James. Why'd you have to ...?"

A crackle of brush and cheering cut off his words and pulled him back. Not far away the color sergeant was waving the tattered flag. Colonel Chamberlain limped past looking neither right or left, just staring ahead, deep in thought. Jeremiah could see Sergeant

76

Clark coming up the hill on the other side of the bush with others in the regiment escorting prisoners.

"Spooner, you there?" Clark called.

"Yes, Sergeant," he answered quickly.

"What the hell you doing?" Clark paused, staring at him.

"Nothing." He quickly got up, picking up his musket.

"The colonel wants us back to our original position to hold the top of this damn hill we just won. Come on." Clark headed away, joining the others heading up the hill.

Jeremiah stared after them a moment, mumbling to himself. "Damn this war anyway. God forgive the fat politicians who started it." He paused and looked one last time at James's body by the bush. "Bye, James. Looks like we ain't going fishing no more."

He headed off up the hill after Clark. This did not feel like any great victory. He hoped no one would notice his tears.

Rienzi: Right From the Horse's Mouth

Everyone knows what a near disaster Cedar Creek was by now. Don't look so shocked that a horse is reaching out mind-to-mind and talking to you. Take a deep breath and listen if you want a firsthand—or should I say firsthoof account. Must say at first, I don't know why you are loitering around officers' horses. Makes me wonder if you can be trusted. But then, obviously, you are in uniform so must belong here. Assigned to stable duty perhaps? All right. Don't panic. I'll introduce myself first.

I'm known as Rienzi and belong to General Phil Sheridan. Heard some rumors that my name might be changed to Winchester because of my part saving the day. I was born in Michigan near Grand Rapids. I'm a Morgan of the Black Hawk stock known to produce fast and sturdy horses. My black color and white star and fetlocks are inherited. On the farm while I was still a foal, I was always bigger, faster, and more agile than the others. I grew to be just over sixteen hands, which in human measurement is five feet and eight inches at the shoulder, powerfully built with a deep chest, strong shoulders, broad forehead, and what some men call intelligent eyes.

I met the general when I was three years old and he was still a colonel of cavalry. He struck me first as a strange sort of human—a swarthy Irishman with long arms, short legs, and an unforgettable bullet-shaped head. I caught his eye when he passed a corral of remounts of which I was one. Probably because I was more alert and carried my head up proud and moved about with confidence. The next thing I knew, officers of the 2nd Michigan Cavalry camped outside of Rienzi, Mississippi bought me and presented me as a gift

78

to him. He was the one that named me after that town. I supposed we were quite a sight when passing the troops or watching them on review, me being five feet eight at the shoulder and the colonel who stood five feet five in his boots. I heard some of the officers' men assigned to be grooms snicker at "Little Phil" saying he shinnied up his saber to my saddle.

I had no idea at that time that I was going to be involved in this appalling thing men call war. I remember in the beginning, men would sing songs around camp about it. One particular song went, "Way down south in the land of traitors, snapping turtles, and alligators. Run away, run away, run away, Dixie Boy." I first thought maybe war was like the chase game I played as a foal with other foals my age or at worst stallions fighting over a mare. In those first two years with the colonel, I learned all about war. There was the terrible thunder of artillery, the crackling of muskets that hurt my ears, the shouting and screams, but I grew accustomed to it. There were the horrible smells of fear, blood, and death that I forced myself to bear. And there was the pain when a bullet grazed or struck flesh. Though wounded a few times, I never failed the colonel and was still with him when he became a general. I was his favorite. When they were available, he sometimes brought me apples or carrots. He would pat my neck and on occasion would talk to me as if I were a person.

Then there came the long day at Cedar Creek I am telling you about. My reins were tied to a fence, where I waited with other horses and was switching my tail nervously. It was at the headquarters in Winchester in a house belonging to a family named Logan. The general had returned from a strategy conference in Washington, from what officers said near me, and planned to sleep late, believing his army was camped safe along Cedar Creek twelve miles away. But I could smell gunpowder in the air, despite the fog that morning, and hear thunder start in the distance. I was familiar enough with how humans fought to know something was wrong.

Next thing I knew, the general and his staff were coming out of the house and mounting up. He was still wearing his formal dress uniform from his visit to Washington, and that included a regulation kepi with two crossed silver swords inside a gold wreath instead of his familiar black porkpie hat. We all cantered through Winchester. There many of Winchester's female population kept shaking their skirts at us, threw dirt and stones, and were otherwise noticeably disrespectful in their conduct.

At Mill Creek, just outside town, the general picked up his prearranged escort, three hundred troopers from the 17th Pennsylvania Cavalry. I knew their identity from being acquainted with several of their officers' horses. By now the racket from the south was an unceasing roar. Then something strange happened. The general hauled on the reins to stop me. He then dismounted and put his head to the ground, Indian-style, to listen. I knew there was no longer the shadow of a doubt in his mind—a major battle was underway at Cedar Creek. When he got up, the general looked somewhat disconcerted. I knew by his demeanor and growing anger scent something was terribly wrong about the battle. Then from a handful of frazzled officers the general and I heard the army had been surprised and routed. It was hard to believe. We had seen another routed Union army—or half a routed army—thirteen months earlier at Chickamauga, but at least then we had been present and in the midst of the action. Somehow, while he was still sleeping and I was resting with the other headquarters' horses, a Confederate force had fallen on his own army at Cedar Creek.

I knew his first thought would be to regroup outside Winchester for a last-ditch stand. We both knew the ground well. But he moved me on, walking at a measured pace while he mulled over what to do. I knew he was in the habit of meeting a challenge aggressively, and we were well-matched in that respect.

Then he mounted me quickly, and with us tearing along at a full gallop, we were quickly fifty yards ahead of our escort. At Newtown a few miles south of Winchester, we found a field hospital, ambulances in abundance, and wounded men all around. There we left most of our cavalry escort to act as a rear guard. Then he spurred me toward the ragged sound of distant battle. The horse of our orderly, carrying our headquarters' swallowtail flag of red and white with the crossed saber insignia of the cavalry, had a hard time keeping pace with me.

I headed to the front at a gallop through the brilliant Indian summer, every leg muscle burning with the effort. The noise of battle seemed to increase with every stride. I felt warm all over and began to sweat. Soon we came upon the first signs of the disaster. We were forced to occasionally take to the fields to avoid a tangle of wagons on the roadway, me jumping over several fences. With a pull on the reins, the general slowed me down to an easy canter and waved his campaign cap at the knots of men huddled around improvised campfires, heating coffee.

"Come back, boys!" he shouted. "Give 'em hell, goddamn 'em! We'll make coffee out of Cedar Creek tonight! Face the other way! We're going to kick those fellows out of their boots!"

One dismounted infantry colonel, demoralized by the rout, shouted back, "The army's whipped!" and continued running.

"You are," the general scoffed, "but the army isn't."

With a quick kick, he put me back into a gallop, and we continued south.

Coming over the rise of a hill through woods, we suddenly confronted the appalling spectacle of a panic-stricken army—hundreds of slightly wounded men, throngs of others unhurt but utterly demoralized, and baggage wagons by the score, all pressing to the rear in hopeless confusion. Their mingled scents of fear hit me like a physical force over the smell of burned powder.

Spurring me onward, I galloped along as the general waved his hat so the troops would see him. Some kept running. But a rolling sound of cheering followed us. I was well lathered with sweat by then. We crossed the road and soon caught sight of another group of soldiers, which I realized was acting as the broken army's rear guard. From being over the road before, I realized we were three miles north of Cedar Creek. Another general greeted us with the words, "My God, I'm glad you've come!" He had to shout over the din.

The general took a verbal report, then nodded and spurred me on. He had me jump over a hastily built barricade of fence rails, followed by the other general. Then the general turned me abruptly to face what remained of the army. It was such a sharp turn, I reared a little, but it was a good show of agility.

"Men, by God, we'll whip them yet!" the general roared. "We'll sleep in our old tents tonight!" At my general's words, the formerly downcast soldiers shouted, cheered, and stamped their feet in approval.

With a flourish of regimental flags welcoming us back to the field, we galloped on, our presence restoring confidence. I needed little prodding, though white foamy sweat stained my glistening ebony coat, my mouth foamed around my bit, my lungs felt on fire, and exhaustion nipped at my heels. From my back the general went about stopping the rout and organizing his troops. For me it all passed in a blur of action with little pauses for rest. I'm glad to say by midafternoon the Confederates were in retreat.

Lastly, I must say the general's timely arrival and inspirational leadership had turned a certain defeat into a momentous Union victory. But he could not have done it without me. Now, cleaned up, watered, and fed my ration of grain, I get to rest for a while until the next emergency crops up. I see you are leaving, now that a sergeant has called you. I wish you well.

The Crucible

*War! Nothing but the final infinite good, for men and God, can
accept and justify work like that!*
—Maj. Gen. J. L. Chamberlain

The Battle at Chancellorsville was a blood-stained recent
memory for most of the men in the Army of the Potomac. In the vast
city of tents, the camp of the Twentieth Maine was quiet, the mood
depressed, despite the promise of a fine May day the balmy dawn
offered.

Only the low talking of men, the clatter of mess kits, and an
occasional cough intruded on Lieutenant Colonel Joshua Lawrence
Chamberlain's thoughts as he walked toward the regimental
headquarters tent with a tin cup of strong coffee in his hand. Thirty-
four and graying at the temples with a flowing mustache, he moved
slower than his usual gait. Yet there was nothing casual about his
erect posture. He was trying to enjoy the morning with thoughts of
his wife, Fannie, and the children at home in Brunswick,
endeavoring to keep the war at bay just a little while longer. The
garden in the front of his Federal-style Cape Cod on Potter Street
would be showing the first hint of green with snow bells and crocus
pushing their colorful blooms to the sun. Fannie would be hard-
pressed to keep six-year-old Daisy and four-year-old Wyllys from
picking them. The college students he once taught would be
preparing for final exams, many eyes drifting out the window to the
new greens. Spring was long in coming in Maine and meant to be
enjoyed after a snowbound winter. Here it was so different, with

trees newly leafed out already and songs of mockingbirds drifting on the breeze.

However, more was drifting in the spring breeze than bird song. Change was in the air. The war pressed in on his thoughts once again. Promotions were coming in. Their old commander, Colonel Adelbert Ames, a tall, irascible, mustachioed twenty-seven-year-old, had been promoted to brigadier general. Ames was leaving tomorrow to report to General Howard of the 11th Corps and take command of the 2nd Brigade of the 1st Division, the German immigrant troops that broke and ran at Chancellorsville.

The 20th Maine had been forced to sit out that battle in quarantine. They had been hit with smallpox from contaminated vaccines that cost the lives of four men and infected eighty-four. It had all been a nightmare. He had been left in command of the quarantine camp while Ames got a temporary assignment on Meade's staff, since there was no need for all officers to remain in the camp. He had tried to go on another assignment himself, but there were no more openings. He did not begrudge Ames his good luck, though to be stuck in a quarantine camp had been an experience he never wanted to repeat. He had managed to get the regiment gainfully occupied guarding the telegraph lines from the front to headquarters, but it was ignominious duty. The boys wanted to fight. They had been in the army since September, taken about all they could stand from the martinet Ames, and had nothing to show for it except being trapped on Marye's Heights at Fredericksburg for thirty-six hours, having made their advance at dusk.

They were out of quarantine now, but moral was at rock bottom. Lawrence shook his head and gazed off at the distant Blue Ridge Mountains, thinking again of spring to push away the gloom of camp. The mountains were showing green in the blue-hazed distance. A mockingbird called from the branches overhead as if announcing the rebirth of life itself. It was all putting him in a dreamy nostalgic mood.

"Colonel," Tom's voice broke into his spring reverie. He turned to find his younger brother right behind him in his new second lieutenant's uniform. An enthusiastic twenty- one-year-old ex-store clerk with a wreath of whiskers that joined in a mustache, the chin clean-shaven, Tom had taken well to army life. Now he was the new regimental adjutant replacing Lieutenant Brown, who was going with Ames. Tom saluted.

"Lieutenant," Lawrence said, returning the gesture.

"Colonel Ames … er … I mean, General Ames wants to see you in the headquarters tent in fifteen minutes. Says it involves reorganizing the senior officers of the regiment."

"Sounds serious," Lawrence returned, feeling his mood go sour.

"It does. I have to round up Ellis and Sam, too." He saluted and left.

Lawrence was almost positive he knew what was on Ames's mind. Ames was a West Point graduate and a tough disciplinarian who demanded the best from his men and the officers who lead them. The men hated him for it, but there was a simple logic in his reasoning. You either became a good soldier or you would die in the field. Officers would either led or be replaced by those who could. There was a problem among the senior officers in the regiment— Major Charles Gilmore. Gilmore was the weakest link in the chain of command. The man embodied all Ames personally hated in politically appointed officers who were out for the glory that went with a higher rank but not willing to lead and take the risks. Gilmore had continuously shirked his duty by being put on sick call every time combat seemed imminent. This was quickly becoming an intolerable situation but hard to prove though Ames and the company commanders were all witnesses to Gilmore's behavior.

Lawrence finished the coffee, taking in the last quiet moments of a pleasant morning, then walked slowly for the headquarters tent he shared with Ames. In a way he was dreading the meeting. He held no animosity toward Gilmore and to a considerable degree felt sorry for him. He found Ames alone in the tent busy at the small field desk. Ames looked up at him with little humor in his intense hazel eyes. "You're early, Colonel, just as I suspected you would be." He forced a smile so fleeting it was almost more of a tic.

He noticed Ames was working on a letter home and not one of the many required reports.

"If my suspicions are correct, this meeting is about …"

"Gilmore," Ames finished his thought for him. They had been together for nine months. Finishing thoughts had become a habit.

No sooner was the name out of Ames's mouth than the other two officers came into the tent: Captain Ellis Spear, the ex-school teacher from Wiscasset, a fragile-looking man with a bearded chin, and Captain Sam Keene, the young bearded ex-lawyer from Rockland. Ellis was an old friend of his, one of his students. Keene was a close friend of Ellis's. The atmosphere was homey yet this time cold. Gilmore was conspicuously absent. The black sheep of this military family.

Ames looked from one to the other. "Gentlemen, as you know, I will be leaving tomorrow to accept command of the Second Brigade in the First Division of Howard's 11th Corps. I want to see to it before I leave that the 20th Maine has senior officers who can lead. We all know there is a problem with Major Gilmore. He may have been sheriff of Penobscot County and politically well connected, but he is unfit for command. Since that close call at Lee's Mills, his confidence has been sadly lacking. That, gentlemen, is not good for the morale of the men who depend on their officers not only to lead but to set an example of coolness under fire. My plan is this: to go on with the promotions of Chamberlain to colonel, Gilmore to lieutenant colonel, and Spear to major. Then I will get Gilmore to resign or transfer, which will put Spear in as lieutenant colonel and Keene in as major, since he is the next senior officer. At that point this regiment will have the proper leadership. Any questions or comments?"

86

"What if Gilmore does not resign, sir?" Keene asked.

"That will be a problem but not an insurmountable one. My guess is his behavior will continue and you, Captain Keene, or you, Captain Spear, will eventually replace him. Let us hope he has the wisdom to cooperate for the good of the men."

A shadow moved on the tent wall. They all looked. Shadows of a bush branch bobbed a little too sharply to be moved by the warm spring breeze. Lawrence was quite sure someone had been listening in, that someone being Gilmore.

It was twilight. Lawrence had finished grand rounds and was on his way to the headquarters tent when he passed Thomas, the aide, leading Ames's horse. God, how he hated goodbyes. He had gotten along well with Ames, spending countless hours studying tactics books and manuals with him, knew this day would come, yet it never seemed to register until now. He knew Ames wanted no fuss. No assembly of the regiment or goodbye speech. He did not feel the need. They both knew it would be a sham anyway. Many of the men still hated Ames's giblets.

Lawrence entered the tent to find Ames packing two clean shirts and a few other essentials in his saddlebags. The general paused in his packing and turned. Their eyes met. "I wish I had your language ability, Colonel. The regiments in the Second Brigade are mostly German immigrants. The ones that ran at Chancellorsville." Ames forced a smile.

"I'm sure you will break them of that habit, General," he said, smiling weakly. Knew he would not see that fleeting smile or that sometimes mischievous twinkle again, the lighter side of Ames the men never knew.

"As I am sure I am leaving the 20th in capable hands, Colonel."

"Thank you, General, for the vote of confidence." He broke eye contact with him and looked at the floor. This was all so awkward.

"You are far too modest, Colonel. You and I have been through hell with this regiment. You have proven you can lead men and have an excellent grasp of tactics. Trust yourself, Colonel. The men certainly trust you. You are one of the finest officers I have known, and you know I do not give such praise lightly. You have also become … a good friend."

Lawrence felt uncomfortable, a twinge in his gut, a small icy hole that came with a growing sense of loss. Loss was a fact of military life, and he knew he should never allow himself to get close to anyone. But sometimes it just happened, especially with roles being reversed as they had these last months, with teacher suddenly becoming student. The army was such a far cry from his academic life, and Ames had been his mentor, his island in a sea of confusion.

There was an uneasy silence, a stillness in which neither of them spoke or moved. It was as if time had frozen and no words could convey what each wanted to say, yet there was a timeless understanding, the passing of a torch.

Lawrence suddenly came to attention and saluted, "General."

Ames came to attention and returned it. "Colonel."

Then they shook hands heartily, and it quickly became an equally hearty short brotherly hug. They broke apart as Thomas and the horse's twilight shadows appeared on the tent wall.

"You take care of yourself and these boys," Ames said, picking up the saddlebags.

"I will, General. You take care of yourself."

Ames left the tent, strapped the saddlebags behind the saddle, took the reins from the silent Thomas, and mounted the bay. Lawrence was at the open flap, the dull candlelight glowing behind him. It was too dark to see Ames's expression, but he knew the general well enough to know there would be a certain sadness in those eyes. He felt an icy emptiness creep in. They had become as close as brothers, a closeness born of the blood and fire of combat.

Ames kicked the horse lightly, and the animal moved off at a brisk walk. He kicked again, and it broke into a trot. Lawrence watched him ride past the rows of tents and the scattered groups of men settling down for the night, this regiment of farmers, lumbermen, and fishermen that called itself the 20th Maine Volunteer Infantry. He knew they had been a bother to Ames and tried his patience beyond the breaking point. Lawrence also knew Ames was proud of the fact that he had turned the survivors into soldiers. He knew Ames would never forget them, no matter what the unsure future held.

———※◦◈———

Lawrence sat at his camp desk with the tent flap open to the balmy May twilight. He was finally finished with his daily paperwork and began to wonder anew how the army ever moved under the glut of paperwork expected from the officers. He had to deal with more now than his days as a professor at Bowdoin, it seemed. The official paperwork for his, Gilmore's, and Spear's promotions had been delayed, but among the first of his new orders was a transfer notice. He would be getting a hundred and twenty men from the 2nd Maine. According to the orders, there was a recruiting error, and these men had signed three-year papers. Those of the 2nd Maine who signed two-year papers had been sent home. He knew the army was presently going through a serious drain in manpower as enlistment times were up with the regiments formed early in the war, a war everyone thought would last only a few months. The 3rd Brigade was losing their two New York regiments, which left only four—the 16th Michigan, 44th New York, 83rd Pennsylvania, and his regiment. With the 20th at just less than half strength, the addition of the remnant of the 2nd Maine would be

89

welcome indeed. Beyond that, he did not give the transfer order much thought.

The quiet evening turned his thoughts toward home. In the candlelight he began writing his younger brother John as a twilight breeze through the open tent flap teased the candle flame to flickering. With Tom, the youngest of his brothers with him as regimental adjutant, John was their mother's last hope for a minister in the family. He was attending Bangor Theological Seminary just across the Penobscot River from the family home in Brewer.

HQ 20th Maine Vols.

May 22nd 1863

Dear John,

I thank you for your kind letters. You may be sure I value them & think of them a great deal. I got acquainted with you in college, somewhat in the way I would with any young man & in addition to some previous & subsequent acquaintance from the time you used to ask for "nickes on capin", to the tree-climbing on Mount Monsummon, makes me believe I am not mistaken in holding a high opinion of you.

I write now chiefly to give one illustration of my good opinion by asking for the pleasure of your society for a few weeks. We shall probably be situated for some little time, so you could find it pleasant to visit us. The season is glorious. Our camp is fine & you would thoroughly enjoy it.

I shall be expecting you soon. You can get a transfer ticket from Boston to Washington, perhaps from Bangor. Then get a pass at Lt. Col. Conrad's 132 Penn Avenue up beyond White House.

Thomas is well & doing well. Mother wrote him a beautiful letter a few days ago. He thinks a great deal of you at home. I am in command here now. We receive the three years men of the 2nd Maine tomorrow morning & that will make us by all odds the best Regt. from Maine. Where is Miss Sae now-a-days? I shall write her when I get a pen that will make the 2nd or 3rd time going over the paper.

Love to Mother & Father & all.

J. Lawrence C.

When he finished, he folded the letter and slid it into an envelope, thinking fondly of John as he addressed it. If John could make the trip, it would be an education in the real world for him.

Lawrence put the envelope in the outgoing mail bag. The bugler blew taps, and the camp began settling for the night. He sat back in the canvas chair, looking out the open tent flap at the night, when he saw a shadowy figure heading his way. The figure became Captain Joe Land, the twenty-four-year-old commander of Company H. As Land reached the tent entrance, he could see several envelopes in his hand.

"Sir, permission to enter," his voice boomed. Land's good friend, Captain Ellis Spear, had described his voice as "like the bulls of Bashan" and was right. "I have mail to go out. Some of the boys were a bit late getting their letters to me, and I know it goes out first thing tomorrow."

"Come on in, Land," he said.

Land had a smile on his strong-jawed face. His dark eyes sparkled with humor. He saluted. "I am truly sorry to bother you after taps. Just couldn't beat the bugler."

He returned the salute. "No bother. Everything all right in Company H?"

"Could be better. We're all tired of sitting around while the idiots running this event try to figure things out, now that our yearly migration to Richmond seems to have hit a snag at Chancellorsville."

He could not help smiling. Captain Land was known for wisecracks. It went with the voice.

"Well, I suspect you'll be hitting the hay early, sir, with our permanent visitors due in tomorrow. Tom says we're getting reinforcements. Second Maine mutineers." He grinned.

"Mutineers?" It was a navy term that took him off guard but held ominous implications.

"I take it, sir, you haven't heard." Land's expression turned serious. He wasn't joking this time.

"I've heard nothing except we are expecting a transfer of three-year men from the 2nd Maine." A resentment over not being told the full story began to burn deep within him.

"Well, from what I hear, sir, we may be in for a load of hurt. Some of them took the news of their staying on real hard and refused to do their duty. Mutinied, sir. Sat down and refused to obey orders. Could be real trouble. They might try to bust a few skulls around here. The army's got them under guard—considers them dangerous after that brigade-wide fight last winter during Burnside's Mud March when they about cleared the field. Must have been something to see. Anyway … Then, sir, the rumors might be wrong. You know how the army is. You can't believe all you hear. Some of these men gossip more than my old Aunt Agnes. Well, good night, sir." Land saluted.

Lawrence returned it. "Good night, Captain."

Land left whistling *Rally 'Round the Flag.* Immediately, he began wondering if it was true. The 2nd Maine men were a contentious lot. The brigade-wide brawl during the January Mud March was proof of that. If the rumors were true, he could be in for the first serious challenge to his ability to command.

92

He had not slept well. He awoke a little before reveille more tired than he had been when he went to bed. He had a few moments to himself after breakfast and walked back to his tent with a cup of bitter black coffee in hand, enjoying the fresh coolness of early morning. He let his gaze drift across the long shadows of the tents to the green canopies of trees, then on up to the distant misty blue mountains, wondering when they would be moving out. He also found himself pondering how long Hooker would remain in command now that he, too, had failed the Union war effort with the defeat at Chancellorsville. God only knew who the next commander would be or when the string of defeats would end. The mood in camp was sour at this point over the inactivity, the Chancellorsville fiasco and the never-ending incompetence of those in high command. He went into his tent.

"Colonel." Tom's yell broke into his thoughts.

He looked out the tent flap and saw Tom running toward him across camp, a paper in hand, looking grim.

"Colonel, sir, we have big trouble," Tom said, coming in and holding out the paper. "The Corn Exchange boys have brought over the 2nd Maine at bayonet point. They're prisoners, sir. About a hundred and twenty of 'em. Waiting over yonder for you on the road at the edge of camp. These here orders … oh … Lawrence … ah … Colonel, sir. They say you're to shoot them if they don't obey. But at this point, I don't think they'd obey Lincoln himself by the looks of 'em."

"What?" He took the paper, read quickly, and saw that Tom was right. It had been signed by General Meade, the 5th Corps commander, a career army man not known for patience.

"Sir, you shoot those boys and you won't be able to go back to Maine when the war is over."

"I know. I wonder if they have thought of that." He looked at his brother.

"Well, sir, you've got to sign for them. That's why I came to get you. Captain Brewer is in charge of the guard and was real adamant about that."

He put the paper on the desk and walked across the camp toward the road, with Tom falling in beside him. He had no intention of following the orders to the letter. There had to be a more humane way of handling this situation. He was tired of seeing common civility shredded by this war. These men had been given a raw deal.

"Sir, what are you going to do about them?"

"I don't know, Tom. I don't know. But I do know I am not going to shoot them. We need them."

They started to pass the picket line where the officers' horses were tied. He paused, picking out his stallion's pale rump among the others. A thought, a plan was forming. Maybe, just maybe he should ride over to Corps headquarters and talk to Meade. Try to convince the general to let him handle the situation his own way, though he did not have a clue yet what that would be. He did know Ames would never approve such an action. It wasn't regular army thinking. But then, Ames was not around anymore. He was now responsible for the regiment. As much as he had learned from Ames, he regarded himself as not wholly regular army in thought and deed. He was a volunteer officer trying to do the best he could and frankly feeling a little insecure at this point. And for the love of God, don't let it show, he told himself.

"Colonel?" Tom's voice brought him back. Tom had gotten ahead of him and turned to face him.

"As soon as I sign for the prisoners, I am going to ride over to Corps headquarters and see if General Meade will let me handle this in my own way instead of arbitrarily solving the problem by shooting first and asking questions later." Lawrence started walking again.

"Do you think that's a good idea? I heard General Meade has got a short fuse. According to General Ames, his staff calls him 'Old Snapping Turtle' behind his back. He might think you're disobeying his orders or challenging his authority and …"

"Tom, I have no intention of disobeying his orders or getting him mad at me."

"Well, I remember just a couple of weeks ago when you went to General Butterfield to get us out of quarantine and … well, the soldiers' grapevine says you're getting a reputation as an officer who will butt heads with the top brass and …"

He gave Tom a sharp look. "That was different."

Ahead, he saw the guards surrounding unarmed soldiers sitting on the road. The mutineers were mostly big men from around Bangor where the regiment had been recruited. They were dusty and haggard-looking in worn uniforms. A captain stood near them in the shade of a tree, his arms crossed over his chest, a sheaf of papers in one hand. As he approached, the captain looked up. All the guards suddenly came to attention, bayonets glistening in the sun.

The captain saluted. "Captain Brewer, the 118th, sir." Lawrence returned the salute. Their eyes met. "Sir, you have to sign for these here prisoners by General Meade's orders," Brewer said loudly enough for the mutineers to hear as he passed over the sheaf of papers and a pencil. "He also said you can shoot 'em if they don't obey your orders and refuse to do their duty. They are nothing but trouble, sir. I'm glad you're takin' 'em."

Lawrence signed the papers and handed them back. He glanced at the mutineers. He could see all eyes were on him—hard eyes, angry eyes.

A voice rose among them, from where he did not see. "They are trying to break us, Colonel. But we ain't broke yet, and we won't, no matter what you do."

Then another. "They ain't fed us in three days, Colonel."

"You men be quiet, or we'll feed you the bayonet," Brewer yelled and shoved the sheaf of papers and pencil into his half-open coat.

"You're dismissed, Captain," Lawrence said in a low voice.

"Sir?" Brewer blinked, confused.

"We won't be needing guards. You are dismissed," he said with an added edge to his voice.

"Yes, sir." Brewer saluted.

He watched Brewer and his guard detail start marching away. The mutineers sitting in the road watched, too. Now they were his responsibility, and he felt quite alone in this situation. Almost found himself missing Ames.

"Colonel, do you think sending Brewer away was wise? Remember what they did at the Mud March? Beat the shit out of ..." Tom started in a low voice.

"Tom, you will get them fed while I go talk to General Meade."

"Huh?" Tom's eyes went wide with shock.

"You heard me. It's easier to deal with men whose stomachs are full, and it will keep them occupied for the short time I'm gone." He turned to the men and in a loud clear voice said, "I am Colonel Chamberlain, commander of the 20th Maine. I know you have had a hard time of it. For now, if you will follow the adjutant here, he'll take you over to the cook tent and get you fed. I will be back to talk with you shortly." He turned to his younger brother, who was looking at him as if he had handed him a sack of rattlesnakes. "They're all yours, Lieutenant." Lawrence headed for the horses without looking back.

He heard Tom say, "You fellows follow me if you want to get fed."

When he looked over his shoulder, he saw them getting up and following Tom through camp, all in a strung-out line. The men of the 20th he passed on his way to the horses had paused in their work to stare at the new arrivals. No one dared say a word of derision to

96

the 2nd Maine men. No one dared make a wisecrack. They knew they were looking upon veterans, many of whom had been the first Maine men in the field in 1861, survivors who did not need to prove themselves. The men of the 20th had yet to be in their first real stand-up fight. The closest they had come so far was being pinned down at Fredericksburg on that terrible hill. As to the remnants of the 2nd Maine, they deserved better than they had been getting from the army. If it was at all possible, he would see that they got it.

He found Prince easily on the line. Like all the officers' horses, the dappled gray stallion was kept saddled and bridled, though the girth was loose, and the bridle was hung around the stallion's neck so he could easily nibble his hay when hungry. Lawrence put the stirrup over the saddle out of the way and tightened the girth, noticing Prince's ears flick back, curious.

"We are taking a little ride," he said to the horse as he put the stirrup back down. Then he slipped the bit in place and buckled the throat latch of the bridle, untied the lead, and mounted. Corps headquarters was only about a mile away, but he was pressed for time.

He turned Prince away from the other horses and found acting-Lieutenant Colonel Gilmore heading his way. Gilmore had refused to follow Ames's demand he resign or transfer and was staying on, much to everyone's chagrin. It was all very awkward, but Gilmore did not hold anything against Lawrence. He only complained about Ames being a young upstart pushing his weight around in his quest to be promoted. Gilmore waved and came over. "Sir, where are you headed?"

"Corps headquarters to see about the 2nd Maine. Keep an eye on them for me. I don't expect to be long. Tom is seeing they get fed."

Gilmore looked toward them, blanched. "My God, where are the guards?"

"Don't need them."

"Sir, I don't think that is advisable. You can't trust ..."

"Colonel, they are not going anywhere. It's time to hold out a carrot instead of applying the stick. But if they get troublesome, put a guard on them."

"I don't know, sir ..."

"Just keep an eye on them." He turned Prince away and cantered toward the road.

The 5th Corps Headquarters tent was easy to spot from the new corps flag flying near it, a blue flag with a white Maltese cross, a red five in its center. A few staff officers were gathered around the front of it. He slowed Prince to an easy trot, then a walk. As soon as he stopped, an orderly came and took the bridle. He dismounted and saw a young captain approaching.

"I am Captain Meade, Adjutant of the 5th Corps. How can I help you, Colonel?" The young officer saluted.

He figured he was talking to the general's son. "I am Colonel Chamberlain of the 20th Maine. If General Meade is not too busy, I wish to see him about the 2nd Maine men, who were just transferred to my regiment."

"Yes, sir. One moment." Captain Meade went immediately to the tent and disappeared inside.

Lawrence stood waiting, looking out on the rows of tents, watching the men go about their daily duties. A voice startled him.

"You're lucky to catch him in one of his better moods today." The voice belonged to a tall mustachioed colonel with dark eyes, one of the staff officers.

Captain Meade came out of the tent. "Colonel Chamberlain, General Meade will see you now, sir."

The colonel smiled as he passed and in a low voice said, "Good luck."

Feeling somewhat apprehensive, Lawrence walked into the tent and snapped to attention with a salute.

Meade stood at a field desk full of papers and put down his glasses. He was tall but stood slightly bowed, with a graying full beard and a receding hairline. His sharp eyes, set in a deeply-lined face with a large Roman nose, gave him the appearance of a tired eagle. "Well, Colonel Chamberlain, I thought I was quite clear with the orders on handling the mutineers of the 2nd Maine." The tone bordered on condescension, and the general fixed him with a cold stare, looking him up and down in an appraising manner.

"General, sir, with all due respect, I understand the orders. I have just come to ask your permission to handle this incident in my own way."

The general began to walk slowly around him, his eagle glare boring into him. "You are not a graduate of West Point, are you?"

"No, sir."

"Ah, then, you must be that college professor General Ames told me about." A faint smile crossed his lips.

"Yes, sir. I taught at Bowdoin for seven years. That seems like a lifetime ago now."

"What courses did you teach?" The glare was back but softer.

"Logic, rhetoric, natural and revealed religion, French and German, sir."

"Then I'd say you have quite a lot of experience training young men."

"Yes, General."

"General Ames was quite impressed with you. He told me so while he served on my staff during Chancellorsville. He seems to believe you missed your calling. Why didn't you go to West Point?"

"Sir, I did not feel the peacetime army was the place for me, and I went to Bangor Theological Seminary instead. Had thoughts of becoming a missionary and going to California at that time in my life. But I did not hear the call and became a college professor instead."

The general stared at him in silence a moment, then shook his head. "Well, you have my permission to handle this mutiny as you see fit. But you will make them do duty or shoot them down the moment they refuse. I know Ames must have gone over military law with you. To refuse duty in the face of the enemy is the same as desertion and by army law is punishable by death. Do you understand, Colonel?"

"Yes, General, I understand. Thank you, sir."

"You are dismissed."

"Yes, sir." Lawrence saluted. It was returned and he left.

The moment he was outside the tent he sighed deeply, looked skyward and breathed, "Thank you, God."

He rode at an easy canter back to camp. He found the mutineers lounging, eating and talking among themselves under a couple of trees. He walked Prince toward them. He decided to stay on the horse. It was a psychological advantage.

Standing off to one side, he was glad to see Tom still keeping an eye on them and that Gilmore had joined him. He went over to the two officers.

"Well, sir, what did General Meade say?" Tom asked.

"I have been given permission to handle this as I see fit. Still, there is the option of the firing squad. An option I intend to avoid at all costs."

"I'd keep them under guard and be prepared to use that option," Gilmore warned.

"Major, these are good men, Maine men from a veteran regiment. They like to brawl, but we need that kind of fighting spirit turned to good use. I think things are going to heat up soon in this war. I want you, Gilmore, to see they are assigned the proper clothing. Then assign them in groups to fill out the companies in our regiment. That will break up the *esprit de corps* they have for further rebellion. Tom, go get the roster and assist him."

"Yes, sir," Tom said and ran for the headquarters tent.

100

Lawrence turned Prince away and rode to the center of the line of mutineers, gathering his thoughts. As soon as he stopped the horse, the men ceased eating and talking, and all eyes were on him. Their stirred-up emotions were almost a palpable force, the hate and outrage that strong.

Keep steady, he told himself. *For God's sake, don't let them think you are nervous.* He tightened his hands on the reins and noticed that his knuckles were white.

"Colonel, we was cheated by a no-account recruiting officer," a thin man said. "He tricked us into signing three-year papers."

"We didn't sign up to serve with any other regiment but the 2nd Maine, and they've gone home," another man called out, his tone venomous.

"Colonel, what you going to do about this?" a powerfully built six-foot private demanded.

"I understand your feelings. This whole affair has been handled badly by the army," Lawrence started.

"You got that damn straight, sir," the big private said.

"I know the fine reputation of the 2nd Maine. But I have no choice in what I have to do. I cannot very well treat you as civilian guests of the regiment. I will put you on duty as I am under orders to do. You will be treated as soldiers should be treated. You will not lose any rights by obeying orders." He shot a quick glance to the side, saw Tom with the roster and a pencil in hand next to Gilmore. "You have my promise that I will personally see what can be done about your claim. I will write Governor Coburn on your behalf and the War Department. For now, you will be entered on the rolls of the 20th Maine. I'll be honest with you. We need you. We are down to less than half strength. We need experienced soldiers who can fight. We lose another battle like we did at Chancellorsville, and we may lose this war. Any day I expect we will break camp to hit Lee. Those of you who want to join us in what may be the last fight, go give your names to Major Gilmore. He'll assign you to your

101

companies and see you get your rifles back. Those who continue to refuse their duty will be put under guard and face court-martial. If General Meade has his way, that could mean the firing squad." He paused. "And, gentlemen, I'll certainly appreciate it if you join us in ending this rebellion. Then we can all go home."

He turned Prince away from them and headed back to Gilmore and Tom. "Gilmore, any man who refuses duty, I want him put under guard."

"Yes, sir," Gilmore said, seeming more relaxed.

Lawrence turned in the saddle and looked back at the mutineers. Many were putting their plates down, getting up, and heading toward Gilmore and Tom.

"I don't believe it," Gilmore said.

"The carrot does work, Major. We will apply the stick only if needed." He turned Prince back to the other horses on the picket line.

"Sure wish Ames thought that way," Tom cracked behind him.

He found himself smiling at his younger brother's words and felt relief wash over him. He hoped it was not premature.

⊷•⊶

Ten of the 2nd Maine men refused duty and were kept with the regiment under guard to await court-martial. On May 28, the First Division broke camp and moved to guard the fords of the Rappahannock. They did so without their commander, General Griffin, who had taken ill. The First Division was put under the temporary command of General James Barnes.

Lawrence rode at the head of the long column of the 20th Maine. He sensed a new campaign was starting. The march ended with the regiment taking up a position to picket the riverbanks at the United States Ford with the rest of the 3rd Brigade strung out about eight miles. On the opposite bank were the Confederate pickets.

The soft delicate greens of May soon became the darker green of thick early June foliage, with the hot sunlight irradiating it as mockingbirds sang in the branches. Orchards hung heavy with ripening fruit. He could not help thinking of home, that it would only be like mid-spring instead of early summer. The balmy, relaxed days made the mood along the river decidedly friendly.

Lawrence heard from Tom that when no officers were around, the enlisted men of both sides had an agreement not to shoot one another as long as no one tried to cross the river. They all went swimming and fishing together and talked things over, even meeting midstream to trade coffee, tobacco, and newspapers. Sometimes exchanges took place in small wood boats with paper sails. He did nothing to discourage the fraternizing. It was a good way to keep an eye on the enemy.

Then one day the men discovered their Confederate friends had gone. On June 6 the brigade moved farther along the Rappahannock, and the 20th Maine ended up guarding Ellis Ford. Tension grew with the distant thump of cannons down the river. Rumors said the 6th Corps had crossed. June 9 brought news of a cavalry fight at Brandy Station. The army headquarters at Falmouth seemed to be nervous and nearly drove Lawrence to distraction, calling for reports every four hours. General Hooker sent out orders. Everything observed across the river day and night was to be reported. Even nothing could mean something in Hooker's mind. It put everyone in an extreme state of anxiety.

After sending off a late evening report, Lawrence was trying to drop off to sleep when he heard some banging that sounded like rifle shots. Too tired to move, he listened longer, hoping it was not an emergency brewing. There were hurried footsteps.

"Captain Clark, turn out the company!" Tom yelled.

Confusion reigned, with officers yelling and men running. He sat up in his cot.

He heard Tom yell again. "Why the hell didn't you give the alarm? There must have been a hundred shots fired!"

Lawrence put his feet over the side of the cot and pulled on his boots.

"We didn't hear a thing," someone answered.

There was silence for a moment.

Then irascible young Captain Atherton Clark bellowed, "A hundred shots my ass! For Christ's sake, Tom, it was only a couple of mules off to our right that got to kicking around a pile of empty hardtack boxes. Go back to bed."

There was some laughter and grumbles. He could not help smiling in the darkness as he pulled off his boots and lay back on his cot.

Rumors and false alarms became all too real. At sunset on June 13, the 20th Maine pulled away from Ellis Ford to join the rest of the 1st Division at Morrisville. The red sky promised clear weather, but with it came a brutal humid heat. The early morning coolness didn't last as the regiment started out in the 5th Corps column the next day. Heat rose with the sun.

Lawrence watched the dust rise up ahead, marking the progress of the troops. It reminded him of the march to Antietam. By midmorning, the pace and the dust began to take a toll on the men. Gasping and staggering, they started to fall out of line to collapse on the side of the road. He knew, as always, they would try to catch up in the night, but he worried just the same.

He rode back to them as they fell out of line to make sure the new orders were carried out. To each man who could not continue the company commanders were to give a slip of paper with his unit on it and permission to catch up later. He was glad to see all were complying.

By noon, there was no breeze. The sun beat down unmercifully, and dust hung in choking clouds. Out of desperation, some of the men put leaves in their caps to keep cooler or cut leafy branches to stick in their knapsacks and hang over their heads to create some shade. What was left of the regiment took on the appearance of a walking forest.

Even up on Prince, he felt as if he was suffocating slowly, and his shirt was soaking wet under the coat he wore half-open. He wished he could strip down to his trousers and ride along bare-chested, but that was out of the question, as it would be considered behavior unbecoming an officer. He thought of dismounting and walking, but it would be too tempting to stay under a tree for a while. He did not want to lag behind, so he pushed on.

When his throat became unbearably dry, he pulled the horse off the road and paused to take a few swallows of warm water from his canteen. He had nearly reached the limit of his endurance when they went into bivouac at Catlett's Station. By then he found he was missing almost half the regiment. Through the night most caught up, and early morning found the army on the move again.

Though the pace was exhausting, most were in good spirits. The main complaint was the lack of mail. Because of the great distances they were marching, the supply wagons carrying the mail had not caught up. He was hoping for letters from his wife and John as well as the paperwork on the promotions.

As the sun climbed higher, baking the land until the distant mountains shimmered, Lawrence's thoughts turned to the brutal, unforgiving heat. Water was becoming scarce, and that began to worry him. At every available trickle of a stream or scum-covered pond, he saw horses and mules drinking, while men gathered to fill canteens. He looked back through the haze of dust at the regiment and saw a repeat of the day before. What was left of the 20th had again become a walking forest.

A headache from the glare and heat began to pound behind his squinting eyes. Even his teeth felt gritty from the dust. He pulled Prince off the road into the shade of a huge chestnut tree and took a drink of water from his canteen, wishing he could will the sun to drop below the horizon. He took only a few swallows and saved the rest, hoping the regiment would find a farm with a well soon. He did not trust the water in scummy pools. He did not feel like swallowing a pollywog along with the water. God knows what else was living and growing in the green scum.

A dusty group of horsemen approached from the direction of the head of the column. As they drew closer, he spotted the brigade flag carried by one of the riders. He recognized the commander, the robust Colonel Vincent, with his bushy mutton chop sideburns. The colonel was dust-streaked but apparently not suffering as much from the heat. Lawrence put his canteen back on the saddle and saluted as Vincent and his staff pulled under the tree next to him.

"I've come to see how my newest regimental commander is doing," Vincent said cheerfully.

"Tolerable, sir. This heat …" He shook his head.

"This heat is hard on all of us, but I imagine it is hardest on you fellows from Maine, not being used to it."

"Yes, sir. We have some hot summer days but nothing like this. Right now it would be more like late spring. Lilacs in bloom, fruit trees starting to set."

Vincent nodded. "How are the 2nd Maine boys adjusting to their new home?"

"From what my company commanders have reported, they are settling in. A few are still grumbling. I've done what I can for their case. Wrote the governor and the War Department. But with the mail being delayed, I don't know where anything stands. I've got ten hard cases under arrest. I hope they will turn around, but I don't know."

"Any luck in finding a surgeon to replace Dr. Monroe? A shame he quit after the epidemic."

"No, sir. I'm hoping my young brother, John, can visit for an extended period. Maybe help our hospital steward if we see any action. Again, I won't know for sure about any of this until the mail arrives. So far Dr. Townsend of the 44th New York has been kind enough to help with our sick and footsore."

"If your brother joins us, you might consider letting him borrow the stallion and find yourself another horse. I know he's been skittish since taking that hit at Chancellorsville. You never know when the shooting will start at this point. Colonel Rice mentioned to me this morning he'd let you borrow his spare horse, a steady gelding. Can't have your stallion bolting on us and carrying you off the field at an inopportune moment."

"Thank you for your concern. I will follow your suggestion, sir. I seem to have bad luck with horses. Colonel Rice is very kind. Give him my compliments if you see him before I do, sir."

"He'll probably ride over with the offer later today or tomorrow. Sooner if it looks like a fight is brewing. You take care of yourself, Colonel. I need all my field officers. I think this next fight will be important, one we can't afford to lose."

"Yes, sir."

Vincent rode on down the line. Lawrence watched his commander for a moment, then joined what was left of the 20th heading for the front of the line. The men moved as if in a heat-induced trance.

By late afternoon they passed Manassas Junction and marched through the old Bull Run battlefields. He looked over fields more like a desert, the parched soil uncultivated, the land covered in thick weeds, air stifling with dust. The crisp pungent odor of pennyroyal rose with the heat and seemed to be everywhere. Worst of all was the debris that still littered the area: skins of dead horses and mules, old shoes, broken muskets, canteens. The elements had weathered away the shallow graves, partially exposing bones and rotting clothing. Skulls grinned up at them from several dusty depressions. Not an encouraging sight considering how close they could be to combat themselves.

When he turned in his saddle to look to the rear, he could see clouds of dust following the column. Enemy cavalry? *Perhaps this portends a little sport by morning.* A third Bull Run. Just past the battlefield, they bivouacked for the night. It was hard to get up the morning of June 17, and Lawrence certainly had no enthusiasm for another day of hard marching.

When he went after breakfast to meet his aide, Sergeant Thomas, who was supposed to be waiting with Prince, he found Thomas holding the reins of a well-built chestnut gelding standing next to another man. Colonel James Rice, a year younger than himself with expressive dark eyes and equally dark hair and beard, smiled pleasantly the moment they made eye contact. A graduate of Yale and a fine volunteer officer, he was known to always be concerned for the welfare of his men and was sometimes criticized for being too easy on them. In battle, he had the reputation of being excitable, and it had gained him the nickname "Old Crazy."

"I thought now was as good a time as any to get my spare horse to you so that when John arrives, he can ride your stallion. You'll need a calm horse anyway if we run into the Rebs before then," Rice said.

"Thank you, Colonel," Lawrence said, approaching the gelding. "Did Colonel Vincent warn you of my bad luck with horses in combat? I'd hate to see anything happen to him."

"Colonel, don't worry about it. I won't hold it against you should the horse get hit. I don't like to name them for that reason. And I try not to get too attached to them. Doesn't always work, though. That one came with a name. Albany. He's good and steady when the bullets start flying. Doesn't even blink."

He mounted the gelding. "Thank you again, Colonel."

"You are very welcome. Ride him in good health, Colonel. You'll find he has no bad habits. I'll be back to visit you later to see how you two are getting along." Rice turned his horse and rode away toward his forming regiment.

108

"Sir, we'll keep Prince ready for your brother when he comes up. He'll be back with the ambulance while we're marching if you want to check on him."

"Thank you, Sergeant," Lawrence said. He turned the gelding toward the assembling regiment, feeling a little lightheaded. The sweat was dripping down his back even though he had not done anything strenuous.

Out on the road the sun beat down unmercifully on the marching blue columns. The men toiled along mile after mile in a humid heat that seemed worse than the day before. His headache returned. By early afternoon, he began to feel somewhat dizzy, and a weakness gripped him. Then his leg muscles began to cramp. Thinking he could do with some water, he pulled the gelding off the road, dismounted awkwardly, and took the canteen off the saddle. The warm water did little to refresh him. He finished what was left in the canteen, strapped it back on the saddle, and stood leaning against the gelding, not sure if he had the strength to mount. *Maybe I should walk the cramps out of my legs first.* He started walking with the horse alongside the regiment.

Lawrence looked at the men and tried to spot Gilmore, but the acting lieutenant colonel was nowhere to be seen. The dust hanging in the stifling air obscured much of the view further down the line. There was little talking. It took too much effort. The leaves on the fresh branches they cut earlier for shade were beginning to wilt in the heat. *Think of something cool. Snow in deep drifts, autumn mist on the Penobscot River, icy trout streams, anything.* But his head pounded, and his dry throat felt as if it was coated with half the road. It was an effort to put one foot in front of the other. His legs began to feel as if they were made of lead. *Maybe I should get back on the horse.*

He stopped, gripped the reins and a handful of mane, grabbed the cantle of the saddle, put his left foot in the stirrup, and swung himself up with great effort. Halfway up a debilitating weakness overcame him, and his heart raced wildly. Peripheral vision became blurred. Then everything seemed to collapse into a dark center. His left leg buckled, and he lost his balance. He hit the ground in an undignified heap to the rattle and clank of his sword scabbard.

Through the darkness came Captain Clark's shout, "Christ, the colonel's down. Lewis, get Gilmore and the adjutant."

"Yes, sir." Lewis's voice was followed by the sound of running feet and the clatter of equipment.

He was barely aware of Clark turning him over and several others around him. An arm was suddenly under his shoulders, propping him up in a sitting position. He was cognizant of his head dropping, his chin resting on his chest. A hand touched his forehead.

He heard Clark's voice again. "He's burning up with fever. Colonel, can you hear me?"

He tried to speak, but only a moan came out. Then all was muffled, voices and sounds spinning into a blackness he did not want to enter but was powerless to stop.

Lawrence was first aware of a cold wetness on his forehead, chest, and arms. Someone was wiping his skin with a cloth dipped in very cold water. The touch was gentle—a woman—but she did not speak.

At about the same time, more of the world was returning. The whisper of a breeze through an open window, a rooster crowing, a dog barking outside, the smells of roses and clean linen. His head felt heavy, but at least the blazing headache was gone. Everything else ached: muscles in his lower back, arms, and legs; cramps in his lower abdomen. The light on his closed eyelids told him it was day, but what day and where? The cloth was gone. He heard the cloth slosh in water. The coldness was suddenly on his chest again, then his arms.

An impossible thought surfaced in his fever-muddled mind. A word formed. A name. He croaked hoarsely, "Fannie?"

Slowly, he opened his eyes. A woman about his age sitting on his left in a wooden chair froze with the wet cloth in hand. She was thin with high cheekbones and wore her auburn hair pulled back in a bun. Her hazel eyes were intelligent and large. She was wearing a dark blue dress with tiny white flowers printed on it and a white apron.

"Welcome back to the land of the living, Colonel. You gave us an awful scare."

He was too weak to sit up. He had to be satisfied with looking around from where he lay propped up on three feather pillows. He found he was unclothed to the waist and minus his boots. His coat, shirt, cap, and sword belt were on a chair against the wall by the foot of the bed, his boots next to it. He was in a tiny bedroom with a single window on his right. From what he could see of the view outside, the bedroom was on a second floor. Next to the woman was a nightstand on which sat an oil lamp, basin of water, pitcher, and glass.

As he focused on her, she spoke again. "I am Clara Sullivan. Your men left you here yesterday. My husband, Hiram, and I are Union sympathizers, so don't fret."

Her words slowly registered in his feverish mind.

"Just stay where you are. The fever is not broken yet." She wiped the cloth down his left arm, then right. "The Union Army's camped just down the road at Aldie. Will probably be there a few days. Your brother and another officer said they will be back to check on you. A Dr. Townsend does not want you to move for a couple of days. He said it was sunstroke."

A shadow appeared in the doorway behind her. He focused on it and found a fiftyish, gray-haired, big-boned man with bushy sideburns looking at him with great concern. "Our patient awake?"

111

"Just barely." She put the cloth in the basin, wiped her hands on her apron, and stood. "I've got some chicken broth on the stove. I think it is time you take a little food, Colonel. Got to get your strength back. Hiram, try to get a little water in him."

When she left, the man came in, sat in the chair, and poured water into the glass. Lawrence watched, his mind clearing a little more. Worries surfaced. "Aren't you taking a chance keeping me here in your house?" he croaked.

The man smiled knowingly. "No one knows you're here. Acres of ground and a couple of woodlots separate me from my closest neighbors. They know our sympathies. Most just tolerate us. A few shun us. I got two sons in the 118th Pennsylvania and one son at the University of Pennsylvania who refuses to get involved in the war." He held out the glass.

"I thank you for your kindness," Lawrence said, reaching for the water with trembling hands.

"Let me help you," Hiram said, lifting him slightly under the shoulders and putting the glass to his lips.

The water was cool and felt good going down. He took a few swallows, then Hiram took the glass and let him down easy.

The big man went on. "I suppose, to be honest, we are taking somewhat of a chance. But Mosby and his men, who have laid claim to these parts, have not proved themselves a threat to us. Besides, it's my duty to help where I can. You were in pretty bad shape when they brought you here. Was afraid you wouldn't make it by the way that army doctor was talking. It's a shame they push you boys the way they do. How the hell do they expect an army to fight when half of it ends up along the road with sunstroke?"

Lawrence smiled weakly. "A lot of the officers and men wonder the same thing. Me included."

Clara came in with a bowl of soup, a thick slice of white bread spread with butter, and a glass of lemonade on a tray. "Hiram, I've got to put the rest of supper on. Would you mind assisting the colonel with his meal?"

"Not at all, darling."

She took the cold compress off his forehead. They both helped him to sit up, propped pillows under him, and placed a cloth napkin on his chest. Then Clara left and Hiram started spoon-feeding him slowly, trying not to spill. "I haven't been a nurse since my youngest had the measles, so I am a little out of practice."

"You are doing fine," Lawrence said. "A lot better than I could. I wish this weakness would go away. I hate being so helpless."

"Give it time. You were near death when they brought you in. We still have to break the fever."

"I hate to leave the regiment with Gilmore in charge." He swallowed another spoonful of broth.

"Mind if I ask why?"

"He manages to get sick every time a fight looms. He does it this time and Ellis gets command. Ellis is acting major. He is an ex-school teacher friend of mine. But I don't think he's ready, though he'd do much better than Gilmore, being the practical man he is."

"I'd say you are in a bit of a fix," Hiram said, giving him another spoonful of broth.

Lawrence swallowed. "I have to get back as soon as I can. I think any day now we are going to find ourselves in a serious fight. I can't let them go in without me."

"We'll do our best to get you on your feet."

When the broth, bread, and lemonade were finished, he leaned back on the pillow and closed his eyes. Though he did not mean to, he instantly dropped off to sleep.

The next few days he was in and out of consciousness and lost track of time. Slowly, some strength ebbed back, but the cramps hung on as did the fever. He spent his time sitting in the bed or chair, wistfully looking out the bedroom window, wishing he was strong enough to leave, wondering why Tom or Ellis or any of the other officers he knew did not drop by.

Hiram brought him the local paper, and he read it several times. First, he was looking for news and was amused by the different point of view. It mentioned Lee was going to move, bring the war north, maybe go all the way to New York to "give the Yankees a taste of their own medicine." The other times he read it just for something to do to occupy the empty hours.

He tried walking to the top of the stairs and back to the room barefooted on the uncarpeted wood floor in the narrow, dark hall and found it exhausted him and made him lightheaded. When distant artillery thundered over the hills, he grew anxious and more frustrated. The army had moved on and was now engaged. The sound brought him to the window, and he stared intently at the distant blue mountains, listening in silent disappointment.

He was in bed dozing in the late afternoon when a commotion at the front of the house broke into his feverish somnolence. He heard horses trot up and the dog barking. A dismal thought surfaced, a fear from the depths of his mind. Mosby's Rebel raiders. He looked over at his sword belt on the chair. He was about to get up and grab the Moore's revolver from his holster.

Then Hiram said cheerfully, "Go on up, boys. The colonel will be glad to see you, but he's probably napping, so go easy."

Boots clomped up the stairs accompanied by low talking. "Can't wait to see his face when he sees you," came Tom's voice.

"I hope he's awake. I'd hate to disturb him." It was John.

He felt his heart race. John had made it. *Thank God.*

"I just hope he'll get back before we move out," Ellis grumbled.

There was silence. He could hear breathing at the door and smell pipe smoke. He opened his eyes.

"Lawrence!" John burst out, rushing to the bed with Tom and Ellis walking in slower. John had let his wavy hair grow a bit long, below his collar, but was clean-shaven.

114

"John, it's so good to see you," Lawrence said weakly. They shook hands, then managed to hug.

"God, sir, you look like something the cat dragged in. How are you feeling?" Ellis said through teeth clenched on the pipe stem.

"You should talk, Major," Tom shot back. "You don't look so spry yourself."

"I think I'm out of danger. Still weak and have a fever. What's been happening? Catch me up on what I've missed." He looked from one to the other.

"Well, I'm a member of the Christian Commission now, and on the way down I stopped in Washington to help out at one of the hospitals. Oh, Lawrence, the suffering was unbelievable. I wrote letters home for the boys, read the Bible, helped out where I could," John said. "I made my way out here through country infested with Confederate raiding parties. Thank God your old commander, General Ames, sent an escort with me to your camp. He sends his compliments, by the way. I still want to see what the army and this war are like before I go back to class at the seminary. So far, I'll tell you, that ride out here was quite an experience. Never knew if Mr. Mosby would come riding down on us."

"Well, I'm thankful you made it, John." Lawrence looked at Ellis and Tom.

Ellis Spear, normally a frail-looking man, did not look good at all.

"I heard the artillery the other day. What did I miss?"

"We went on a little expedition with the 1st Division and finally saw the back side of Confederate uniforms," Ellis answered and took a draw on his pipe.

"Ellis, you look a little pale yourself," Lawrence said, concerned.

"Malarial fever hit with diarrhea the same day you collapsed." He blew smoke as he talked.

"Why aren't you in the hospital? You should be in bed."

115

"Gilmore has monopolized that resort as usual. I couldn't go without discredit. Someone has to keep the regiment running, with you out of action."

"I take it that Gilmore did not command in this fight?"

"No, he fell out of the march all the way to a hospital in Baltimore on the twenty- first," Ellis came back coldly.

"Colonel Vincent asked Lieutenant Colonel Freeman Conner of the 44th New York to take temporary command of our regiment. He's a fine officer—experienced, cool, and careful of his men. Did a good job with us," Tom added.

Lawrence noticed a sad, distant look on Ellis's face.

"Casualties?"

"Three wounded and one died in my company. Cannon shot came bounding straight through the company over a stone wall we took cover behind. Corporal John West lost his leg and life to it. Buried him near the stone bridge at Goose Creek." He looked at the floor. "I recruited that boy. Promised his family I'd watch out for him." He sighed deeply.

"Ellis, it's not your fault." Lawrence could see it was causing Ellis deep emotional pain, the kind only time could heal. The same pain he knew he'd feel soon when he'd be giving orders that got men killed. This time as the commander of a regiment, he'd be ordering death on a far greater scale in crucial, agonizing decisions, all part of the loneliness of command Ames spoke of during their late-night study sessions. It left him shaken. He would write West's family.

"On one level, I know that, sir, but a proper burial has done little to diminish my feeling responsible for him … and his death."

"Well, sir, try to look at the bright side. At least we chased the Rebs to the other side of the Blue Ridge, so Corporal West did not die in vain," Tom said. "Too bad you missed it, Colonel."

"Well, I don't want to miss much more. I think I'll try to get back to camp tomorrow, even if I end up lying around the headquarters tent. Might as well stay in bed there as here. I have imposed on these kind people long enough."

"You sure, sir?" Ellis said, a worried look suddenly clouding his face. "That action we saw wasn't a real battle. Just a series of skirmishes. You don't look well enough to travel, let alone fight."

"I know that, Ellis. I know." Lawrence sighed. "I don't think I'm in any shape to ride a horse. Too weak. Would probably slide right off if he broke into a trot. Send over the ambulance tomorrow morning."

"I don't think that's wise, sir. Coming back too early. You need bed rest in a real bed," Ellis protested.

"Ellis, just humor me."

"Sir, at least we won't be going anywhere tomorrow, so he'll have another day of rest. We're supposed to just sit around tomorrow, according to Colonel Vincent," Tom broke in. "Guess they figure we all need to rest up from the excitement."

"I could use the rest, I'll tell you," Ellis said.

Lawrence noticed John was looking at him critically.

"Lawrence, I think you'll be needing more than just another day's rest. You were out cold with a high fever, and your heart was racing to beat the band, according to Dr. Townsend. Sunstroke is nothing to take lightly. It's killed a few of the men, from what he told us. Please reconsider."

"I'm going back to camp tomorrow in the ambulance. I'll probably not move from the tent if I still feel as I do now. Besides, Dr. Townsend is a lot closer in camp."

"Well, we'll see you here tomorrow with the regiment's ambulance, then," Ellis said. He turned to John and Tom. "Boys, let's take our leave and let the colonel get some rest."

John patted his shoulder. "See you tomorrow, Colonel."

"You two stay out of trouble," Lawrence said, smiling weakly.

"Oh, we will. Maybe I'll show John where we made the Rebs skedaddle," Tom said.

"I'd like that," John said and smiled.

"Then maybe I'll give him a rifle and teach him to drill with the regiment," Tom added with an impish grin.

"When pigs fly," John shot back as they went out the door.

Lawrence smiled and watched them file out of the tiny room.

———————

Fully dressed, he walked down the narrow upstairs hall and slowly down the stairs. Unasked, Clara had gone to the trouble of washing his shirt and socks. He was still not feeling well. The cramps hung on as a dull, intermittent pain, and the weakness was still with him, though it was somewhat improved. His lightheadedness told him the fever was not totally gone, and he broke into a sweat easily. Still, he had to get back, force himself to keep moving. He did not want to be an imposition on the Sullivans any longer. He further rationalized his decision to leave knowing that things were heating up in the war. He feared for their safety and his own should Mosby hear they were harboring a Union officer.

He heard Tom, John, and Ellis in the parlor talking with the Sullivans as he reached the bottom of the stairs. John came out of the parlor and looked at him.

"There he is." Ellis joined him in the hallway and quipped, "You still look like something the cat dragged in."

"Thank you, Ellis. You don't look much better yourself," he shot back with a weak smile that Ellis returned.

"Well, Dr. Townsend wants you both to be taking your medicine. Lawrence, he'll be around to see you when you get back to camp," John said.

He walked past them to the Sullivans, who were in the parlor with Tom, and shook hands with Hiram. "Thank you for all you have done. I won't forget your kindness."

"Our pleasure," Hiram said.

Suddenly, Clara stepped forward and hugged him, taking him by surprise. "You take care of yourself. If for no one else, at least do it for your dear Fannie and the children."

"I will, Mrs. Sullivan," he said as she let go.

The Sullivans hung back as he walked slowly down the porch stairs with Ellis and his brothers behind him. He noticed Prince was part of the team tied to the horse-drawn ambulance. As his brothers and Ellis mounted their horses, he turned at the bottom of the stairs toward the Sullivans up on the porch. "Thank you again." He waved.

They waved back. Clara called, "You and the boys will be in our prayers."

Lawrence turned toward the ambulance and saw young Grandville Baker, the regiment's hospital steward, waiting for him.

"Sir, let's get you settled," Baker said. "Want to get out of here before the neighbors send out word for Mosby. On the way over, some farmers gave us the eye. Got a gut feeling they may ride with him at night. You can't trust nobody in these parts. Wish we brought a mounted guard with us."

"That would draw too much attention," Tom called.

"Baker, quit your bellyaching," Ellis added. "Mr. Mosby and his Rangers are cowards that only attack at night. Besides, camp is just a few miles down the road."

Lawrence climbed in with Baker's help and sat on one of the leather upholstered seats that ran the length of each side of the white canvas-covered wagon. He was dizzy and glad to get off his feet.

"Dr. Townsend wants to see you as soon as we get to camp, sir," Baker called, climbing into the driver's seat. "He said he'll be stopping by your tent, and you are to get right to bed."

"Never fear. Once I get back, I won't be wandering far," Lawrence said, stretching out on his back on the seat.

The ride the few miles back to camp near Aldie was anything but comfortable for him. If there was a rut in the road, the ambulance found it. He could not see how any seriously wounded man could survive transportation in this manner. By the time they reached camp, he felt worse than when he had started the trip.

The ambulance pulled up close to the headquarters tent. As Baker helped him out and walked with him to the tent, he noticed the camp was neatly set up along company streets. The army seemed to be halted in mid-campaign. Suddenly, he could not get to bed quickly enough. His energy seemed to be draining with every breath he took. As soon as he entered the tent, he took off his sword belt, coat, and cap, hanging them up on pegs nailed to a board along the tent wall by the desk. He collapsed on his cot without taking off his boots. He had just started to drift off to sleep when he heard someone at the entrance of his tent.

"Sir, I hate to disturb you," Thomas said, "but Dr. Townsend is here to see you. Welcome back, sir."

"Send him in," Lawrence said thickly. It was all he could do to push himself up to a sitting position.

Dr. Townsend, tall, in his thirties with a thin mustache, came in with a small brown bottle and spoon in hand. "Colonel, I am pleased to see you are somewhat better now than we left you."

"That seems questionable," he said and forced a weak smile. "That ride in the ambulance left something to be desired."

"As Captain Spear may have mentioned, I want to start you on some medicine. This is quinine in whiskey. I want you to try to take four doses a day about every three or four hours. Put a spoonful in some water or take it straight. I'm afraid you may have malarial fever on top of the sunstroke, and this will get rid of it plus help break the fever." Dr. Townsend put the bottle on the field desk, grabbed the pitcher of water, poured a little into a tin cup, added the medicine, stirred, then handed the cup to him. "Drink. I want to be sure you get one dose right now. I'll have Sergeant Thomas see that you take the others. We may be in camp a few days, and that will give you a better chance of recovering more quickly. The men in your regiment are deeply concerned for your welfare, Colonel, so

120

please follow my orders. Your health depends on it, as does their morale."

Lawrence nodded, took the foul-tasting medicine, and set the cup on the desk.

"Good. Now I'll take my leave so you can get some needed rest. I can't declare you fit for duty until that fever's gone and your strength is back a lot more than it is at present."

"Thank you, Doctor," he said and lay back on the cot.

He stayed in his tent all the next day and had plenty of visitors. John had appointed himself official nurse and saw that he took his medicine. Ellis took care of the daily paperwork and administrative duties, since he was acting major and in temporary command. On June 26, Ellis came in with orders they would be moving out the next day.

A cup of coffee in hand spiked with the bitter medicine, Lawrence walked to get exercise and build back strength. He met Tom carrying the regiment's papers in a wood box up to a mule-drawn wagon to be left behind with the rest of the baggage.

"You're looking a lot better, Colonel," Tom said, hoisting the box to the tailgate of the wagon, where a teamster took it and placed it in an empty spot.

"I feel a lot better but not one hundred percent. Dr. Townsend will not put me back on active duty yet," he said. "Anything to report?"

Tom turned to him. "Well, we got eleven men under arrest, ten of whom are the hold- out transfers from the 2nd Maine. The other one is Lieutenant Addison Lewis of Company A for being three days late coming back from leave."

"Maybe the transferees will change their minds once the shooting starts." He took a swallow of coffee.

"Sir, you are the eternal optimist."

"Maybe, but men do change with the circumstances. If Lee heads north on another invasion plan like last September, our prisoners may just have a change of heart."

"Don't I wish," Tom came back.

The next morning brought rain and a dampness that went to the bone. Reveille sounded at 0430. After a quick breakfast, the troops broke camp and set off north on the Leesburg Road at 0600, leaving most of the baggage, including shelter tents, behind in the wagon train.

Wrapped in his rubber poncho, Lawrence rode the chestnut gelding at the head of the regiment by the color guard, staring into the rainy haze. He was doing his best to ignore the aches and pains the humidity brought out and the lightheadedness from the remnants of a fever. John pulled up next to him on Prince.

"I don't know what you are trying to prove. I wish you would ride in the ambulance, Colonel. You are not well enough to travel like this. And in this weather the doctor said …"

"John, I will ride like a man," he said, glaring at his poncho-clad brother. Then he felt a pang of guilt at the pained look on his brother's face. John meant well. "I'm sorry, John. I'm not one to give in so easily. I'm not like that shirker, Lieutenant Colonel Gilmore."

"I forgive you. You always were cranky when you didn't feel well. And God forbid I tell you to shirk your duties." John grinned.

Beyond John he noticed another lone rider approaching. It was Colonel Rice. The colonel pulled his horse alongside. "I am happy to see you are up and about, Colonel."

"Thank you, sir, but your good Dr. Townsend has not released me to active duty."

"Well, you gave us an awful fright, and he is cautious. You still look a bit peaked. Why don't you just try to take things slow and easy as you ride. I'll lessen your responsibility and watch over the 20th for you on the march."

"See, I'm not the only one concerned," John broke in.

"Thank you, sir. I appreciate that. John ..." He frowned at his brother.

"Colonel Rice, my brother is being bullheaded. He should be in an ambulance," John insisted.

Lawrence glared at his brother again. "John ..."

"I can go over your head to a senior colonel if I want to, Lawrence. I'm not in the army," John said, cutting him off.

"He's got you there, Colonel," Rice said with a broad grin. "If you get to feeling poorly and want to ride in the ambulance for a spell, no one will hold it against you."

"I'll have to feel awfully sick before I ride again in one of those bone breakers, sir," he said and smiled at Rice.

The column moved out slowly. Rice continued to ride with him and his brothers, occupying himself with a lively debate on scripture with John. Lawrence paid no attention to the exchange, his mind drifting to thoughts of Fannie and the children as he quietly watched the wet Virginia landscape slip past in a dismal rainy haze.

The rain soon turned the roads to mud. He didn't know which was worse—a broiling sun and dust or rain with mud. Each had its own set of miseries. Dust rubbed up blisters as easily as wet leather.

The creeks swelled so the pioneers had to build makeshift bridges of logs at a few points. The column was forced to halt when an occasional team of horses or mules got bogged down in knee-deep mud. The constant stop-and-go began to sap what strength he had. His poncho made him feel as if he were in an oven, and he broke out in a cold sweat. He began to see the wisdom in John's words. *What am I trying to prove?*

Just after they forded Goose Creek, Dr. Townsend rode up to their little group of officers.

"Gentlemen," Dr. Townsend said with a polite nod, then looked at him critically. The doctor pulled his horse next to Lawrence and reached out to quickly feel his forehead. "Colonel Chamberlain, I

123

think it best you ride ahead with John and Tom to Leesburg, find an accommodating residence, make yourself comfortable, and recuperate for a few hours. You can rejoin us when we march through three or four hours from now, if my guess is right on the present progress."

"Think I'll take you up on that," Lawrence said weakly, knowing if he did not rest soon, he would end up face down in the mud.

"You've got to take care of yourself, Colonel," Rice said. "This campaign could turn serious any moment once we find Lee. I know you don't want to miss it. Besides, Colonel Vincent needs all his field officers, and your regiment is shy of most of them."

He nodded and looked at his brothers. "Let's go, boys."

They pulled out of line and rode on the side of the road past the troops slogging along through the mire. They soon left the column behind. In a drizzling rain, they rode for miles through rich farmland to Leesburg. By the appearance of the road, half the Army of the Potomac had already passed through the town.

Lawrence got the feeling there was a great dislike of bluecoats in Leesburg. All the window shutters were closed, and no one was in sight. Not even a dog roamed the street. It was like a ghost town. From the chimney of one house a small Confederate flag flew defiantly, though limp from the rain. He had the overwhelming feeling they were being watched through cracks in the shuttered windows.

"I think we are about as welcome here as a biblical plague of locusts," he said to his brothers, finally breaking the unsettling silence.

John looked at him. "I've got that feeling, too."

"Maybe this ain't such a good idea. Maybe we ought to go to the local inn," Tom suggested.

"What? And end up in a brawl with some drunk Rebel sympathizer," John shot back. "We'll find a nice residence. Let me do the talking. I'm not in uniform."

They rode through most of the town with John in the lead. He suddenly stopped Prince by a white picket fence and pointed to a small sign on it that read: MICHAEL BROOKS, M.D. "This looks good. A doctor certainly won't refuse a sick man."

Lawrence watched John dismount and tie the reins to the fence. Then John walked up the brick path to the colonial-style brick house and boldly knocked on the door. Nothing. Lawrence sat quietly on the gelding, beginning to feel the chill of the rain, and he shivered. *The fever's probably back.* He stared hopefully at the house, saw John knock again. Then the door opened slightly. In the doorway stood a well-dressed stately fortyish woman, her dark hair in a chignon. John immediately took off his hat and spoke to her, gesturing toward Lawrence and Tom. They were too far away for him to hear. He tried to guess by reading the expressions that crossed the woman's face. First a frown, then a forced smile when John handed her something. A teenage girl appeared next to the woman, maybe eighteen or nineteen, thin and delicate with blonde hair. She joined in the conversation. Then the woman motioned to them to come and stepped away from the door. John came back toward them with a smile on his face.

"Colonel, we have been invited for dinner. Mrs. Brooks informed me they are secessionists, but her husband, now a surgeon with the Confederate Army, would not turn away a sick man," John explained upon reaching them. "Besides, I paid for the meal."

"How did you keep her from slamming the door in your face right off?" Tom asked.

"I told her I was from the Christian Commission, and that softened her stance. That and the greenbacks." John came over to him. "Lawrence ... Colonel, you need help?"

"I think I can manage." He slowly dismounted, leaning for a moment against the horse, his legs stiff and numb from riding.

"You all right?" Tom said, coming closer.

"Just need to get the feeling back in my legs." He straightened up and smiled weakly. "Don't want to make a fool of myself by ending up in the mud."

"We're being watched," Tom broke in.

He glanced at the house. The girl was in the doorway holding the door. They all walked toward her up the brick path. The girl pulled the door open wider as they reached it. The moment they stepped into the large entry hall, she closed it quickly behind them as if not wanting the neighbors to see them. Her face was a featureless mask, her blue eyes sharp with resentment.

The entry hall was wide, with an Oriental rug runner over a dark oak floor. The walls were painted a pale golden yellow. At the back of the hall, a white spiral staircase led to a second floor. Oil portraits of ancestors hung on the walls right on up the stairs. To the left, walnut pocket doors closed off a room, and to the right was a large parlor.

"You can hang your rain things and hats on that rack," she said, pointing to a brass clothes rack by the wall. She watched them like a suspicious house cat as they took off their dripping ponchos and hats and hung them up where indicated. Then she forced a smile. "Come with me."

They followed her to the right through the beautifully decorated parlor to a dining room, where the older woman was just finishing adding three Blue Willow place settings to the four that were already down on a long mahogany table. The delicious scents of fried chicken and biscuits came from a kitchen at the far end of the room.

"Have a seat, gentlemen. I am Mrs. Emily Brooks. My daughter is Ann," the woman said, looking at them in an evaluating manner.

126

John instantly took it upon himself to do the introductions. "I am John, as you kind ladies know. This is Colonel Joshua Lawrence Chamberlain and Lieutenant Tom Chamberlain."

"You're all brothers." Mrs. Brooks looked surprised. "I must say, now that I get a good look at you gentlemen, there certainly is a family resemblance. Where are you from, if I may be so bold?"

"Maine, Mrs. Brooks," Lawrence answered. He sat before his legs gave out.

"Ann, honey, check the chicken," Mrs. Brooks said. Ann left for the kitchen. "I must say that explains your manner of speech. I could not quite place it. I've done a lot of traveling up north with my husband but never that far. Mostly Pennsylvania and New York."

In Lawrence's feverish mind, she seemed nervous, forcing a pleasant conversation to avoid sensitive subjects. Looking at the table settings, he wondered who else would be showing up for dinner. It was an awkward situation. He knew it was a great imposition on people who regarded him and his brothers as hated invaders, not to mention the situation of three men in a household that seemed, so far, composed of only helpless women.

"You look a little feverish, Colonel. Let me get you some ice water. Excuse me, gentlemen." She left.

"Ice?" Tom said. It was a rarity that surprised him, too. "Must have a cold cellar here to keep ice in this heat."

They sat in silence. Then Ann came out of the kitchen with six glasses of ice water on a tray. *Strange. There are seven place settings.*

Ann caught his stare as she set down the glasses. "You are confused by the number, Colonel. Well, I did not miscount." Her voice was strained, sharp. "We always keep a place setting for Papa, even though he is away with our brave army seeing to the wounded."

He smiled gently at her as she placed a glass in front of him. "That is a very kind sentiment, Miss Brooks."

"Ann, mind your tone of voice," Mrs. Brooks called from the kitchen, then appeared with a large bowl of fresh peas in one hand and basket of biscuits in the other. "Go tell Aunt Betty dinner is ready, and tell her we have gentlemen guests."

"Yes, Mama," Ann said and left.

"I must apologize for my daughter's behavior. She is her father's pet, our only child, and she resents him being away because of the war," Mrs. Brooks said as she headed back to the kitchen.

Lawrence and his brothers stood as Ann returned, helping an elderly woman into the room. Her white hair was in a neat braided bun. She wore a dark burgundy dress and carried an ebony cane. She smiled graciously, and her dark eyes sparkled with wit from a face free of all but a few wrinkles. "Gentlemen," she said with a nod as Ann helped her into her chair. "I must say I was never expecting guests for dinner ... guests in blue coats. This is a secessionist household. But I always said Emily cooks enough for an army. The girl just doesn't know how to measure portions right. Things have been like that since Flo left thanks to your ..."

Mrs. Brooks cut her off as she came out of the kitchen with a bowl full of carrots. "Aunt Betty, you know Michael would not mind helping anyone who was ill or wounded, no matter what color he's wearing. Introductions are in order. These are the Chamberlain brothers from Maine—John, Joshua, and Tom. Ann, go get the chicken."

Ann cast them a sharp glance and obeyed.

"Personally, Aunt Betty, I prefer not to talk about politics at dinner. It's bad for the digestion," John said and smiled pleasantly.

"And why aren't you in uniform, young man?" the feisty older woman demanded. "You can call me Mrs. Carter. I am the doctor's aunt, not yours."

"Yes, Mrs. Carter. My apologies. I am with the Christian Commission and studying for the ministry at Bangor Theological

128

Seminary," John explained. "I am here visiting my brothers while school is out for the summer."

"My, my, my. You'll say grace for us, then?" Mrs. Carter said, smiling.

John looked at his brothers. "Ah … ah … yes, Mrs. Carter. Would be glad to."

Ann and Mrs. Brooks came in with plates heaped with fried chicken and mashed potatoes with gravy. Everyone sat.

John looked at them, and they all bowed their heads. "Dear Lord, we thank Thee for what we are about to receive of Thy bounty and for the kindness and generosity of the women who share it with those whom they consider to be enemies. And we pray that we may all know the sweetness of Peace once again under Thy merciful guidance. Amen."

"Amen," they all echoed, and the atmosphere seemed less tense. The food was passed, and each took what they wanted, with plenty to spare. Lawrence took a sip of the ice water. It felt so good going down that he wished he had a compress of ice in a towel to put on his forehead. He also wanted to lie on a bed or couch. Serious doubts began to enter his mind about being capable of traveling much farther. He hoped this fine meal would make him feel better.

"Colonel, which brother are you—John, Joshua or Tom?" Mrs. Carter suddenly asked as she cut her portion of chicken.

"Joshua," he said and took a fork of peas. He wondered briefly if Fannie and Cousin D put in vegetables this year or had the handyman do it.

"Joshua is such a strong biblical name. Was my husband's name, too," she went on, picking at her food as if deep in thought.

They all ate in silence for a while. He noticed Tom looking at Ann a little too long with that special hunger of all twenty-one-year-olds. Ann glared back at Tom, then averted her eyes.

Mrs. Carter broke the silence. "Colonel, with what are you afflicted? Nothing contagious, I hope. Ann neglected to inform me.

129

The army is such a breeding ground for all sorts of diseases, from what my dear nephew tells me in his letters."

"Sunstroke, Mrs. Carter. I am recovering from sunstroke," he said and swallowed more water.

"It almost killed him," Tom added.

"Oh, my, my," she said. "I guess our weather is too hard on you fellows from so far north."

"I guess it is," Lawrence returned. As good as the food was, he felt more uncomfortable by the moment over the situation.

"Too bad your government won't leave us alone, let us have our own country, and live the way we want. Then you wouldn't be ill," Ann suddenly burst out, glaring at him.

"Ann!" Mrs. Brooks snapped. "Mind your manners with our guests, or you will have to leave the table. Papa would be so disappointed in you."

"Papa isn't here. Flo's gone, and we have to cook and clean for ourselves," Ann continued. "Now we have Yankees in the house."

"Ann!" she put her hand down hard on the table, rattling some of the dishes.

"That is quite all right, Mrs. Brooks," he said. "Your daughter has the right to express her opinion."

"But it is not proper for a young lady of breeding to behave so," Mrs. Carter added, staring coldly at Ann, who pushed her food around her plate without eating.

"I would be upset, too, if I were in her shoes, Mrs. Carter. I know how emotional some young people can be over a cause they support. I've had a lot of experience with young people, having been a professor at Bowdoin College." He hoped that would help smooth things between the women.

"A gentleman and a scholar. What did you teach?" Mrs. Carter asked, her bright eyes locking on his.

"Several disciplines: logic, rhetoric, natural and revealed religion, French, and German," he replied.

"My, my, my. And what did you do, young man?" Mrs. Carter suddenly turned her attention to Tom, who had just shoved a fork of potatoes dripping with gravy into his mouth.

Tom swallowed hard. "Nothing so grand and intellectual as my brother, ma'am. Was just head clerk in a local dry goods store in Bangor."

A welcome silence fell as they continued to eat, punctuated only by Ann's venomous glances and her fork scraping on her plate. Apparently, Mrs. Carter's curiosity had finally been satisfied.

Once dinner was over, Lawrence and his brothers retired to the sumptuously decorated parlor while the women tended to the dishes. The only thing out of place among the paintings and fine furniture was a small Confederate flag hanging on the massive floor-to-ceiling bookcase. He made himself comfortable in a chair by the open double windows. A deep lethargy gripped him. In moments, he dropped off to sleep.

He was awakened by the heavy footfalls, talking, and clank of equipment of troops passing.

"Sir, let's go," Tom called from the hall.

He heard the rustle of a poncho being put on. He noticed John was already gone from the parlor. He got up a little dazed and headed for the hall, glancing at the massive bookcase, noticing that the flag was gone. *Strange.*

On his way out, he saw Mrs. Brooks in the dining room pulling up the tablecloth. He strode to the archway between the two rooms. "Mrs. Brooks, I want to thank you for your hospitality. I am very sorry we were such an imposition."

"This war is an imposition, Colonel. I apologize for my daughter's behavior. I wish you well, sir."

He nodded and walked out to the hall, took his poncho and cap from the rack, and put them on. Then he went out the door, closing it behind him, thinking what good friends this family could have been under different circumstances. He knew Fannie and Mrs. Brooks would probably enjoy each other's company.

He looked at the shuttered houses of the town, the muddy blue-clad troops slogging along the street in the gray drizzle. *If the war were to end tomorrow, how long it would take to heal the scars on the nation's soul?*

━━━━●━━━━

Twilight was settling over the gently rolling Maryland countryside. Now that the rain had stopped, fireflies blinked their semaphore signals in the wet grass.

Lawrence sat on a rocker in his shirt sleeves on the porch of the Donaldson's two-story white clapboard farmhouse, drinking a glass of cool well water. He was feeling much better. As he watched the rear guard of the 5th Corps march by on the road from Liberty, he hoped Dr. Townsend would pronounce him fit for duty. On the doctor's orders, he had once again ridden ahead on the rout to find a farmhouse where he could rest and recuperate. It was a lot easier in Maryland, where people were friendly toward their Union benefactors. His brothers or other officers rode with him and later returned to the regiment once he was settled.

This farm was owned by a delightful elderly couple, who had gone to bed early after they enjoyed a supper together, talking of family and war news. He was waiting to see if Dr. Townsend and his escort would show, watching the road through the towering sycamores that edged the wheat field in front of the house. The night shadows deepened, and a whippoorwill began to call.

Three horsemen appeared out of the growing darkness and rode up the farm lane, one on the unmistakable gray stallion. Lawrence stood up and walked to the porch stairs. As the riders drew closer, he quickly recognized the other two as Tom and Dr. Townsend.

132

"Well, you seem a lot better," the doctor said, dismounting by the stairs and handing the reins to John. "Let's go in the house where we will have more light."

"We'll wait on our horses here," Tom said. "Got a bunch of news for you, Colonel, so be sure to come back."

He led the way to the small modest parlor lit by a single oil lamp. The doctor examined him in silence, checking his eyes, feeling the pulse in his neck and wrist, touching his forehead, and listening to his chest. Finally, Dr. Townsend asked, "How do you feel?"

"Still a little weak but otherwise quite fit."

"I'd say you can return to duty tomorrow, but take it easy on the march. You get to feeling bad, you pull out and rest."

"That I will, Doctor," he said as they walked out to the porch.

"Well?" Tom asked, still sitting on his horse.

"I'll be joining the regiment tomorrow." He followed the doctor down the stairs to the yard, pausing next to Tom.

"The boys will be glad to hear that, especially poor Captain Spear," Tom said. "He's been sick all this time and handlin' the regiment with the help of Colonel Rice and Lieutenant Colonel Conner. He was feelin' a bit better today, and I 'spect he'll be feelin' a lot better knowin' you're comin' back."

"What else has been going on?"

"No more skirmishing, but we had a problem in the regiment," John broke in.

"Problem?" The first thing he thought was that the 2nd Maine holdouts had started something.

"When we passed through Frederick, the people went wild like they did last September. Some men from the Corps fell out, became involved with the celebration, and got a little drunk," Tom explained.

"A little drunk is an understatement, Lieutenant," Dr. Townsend added.

133

"Well, Color Sergeant Charles Proctor had a little too much. Cussed me and some of the other officers out. We had to relieve him of his position of honor. On the march today, he fell out with the world's worst hangover. The rear guard boys couldn't keep him up, so they left him behind. Listed him as AWOL."

"Who is the color sergeant now?"

"The honor has been passed to the next sergeant in seniority, Andrew Tozier, one of the 2nd Maine transfers," Tom went on and smiled.

"He's a good man, a couple of years older than me," John said. "Talked to him on the march today. He's been through a lot. He was in Gaines Mills, where he lost the middle finger of his left hand, broke at least one rib, and got a bullet in his left ankle, which they never got out. Spent time in two Rebel prisons right after that, too. Got out in a prisoner exchange. Had a hard life before joining the 2nd Maine. His father was abusive and a drunk. Didn't ruin him, though. Nice fellow despite all that."

"Oh, the big news is that Meade is now in command of the army. Our old corps commander. Can you beat that?" Tom went on brightly. "A General Sykes now has our corps. Also, the rumors are true. Lee is going north. Probably in Pennsylvania by now. This next fight is going to be a big one. One we got to win. That's why they're pushin' us so hard."

"Tom, tell him the rest. Give him the papers," John interrupted enthusiastically.

"All right! Will you give me a chance!" Tom reached over and gave his brother a good-natured smack on the shoulder. "I am the adjutant of this regiment. Remember?" He reached into his open coat and pulled out a slightly wrinkled folded paper. "You're official now. This is your commission as colonel. The mail finally came through. Gilmore was made lieutenant colonel, only he ain't here to get his commission. Will have to send it on to the hospital in Baltimore or wherever he's holed up."

"What about Ellis?" Lawrence asked, taking the paper. He folded it and put it in his trouser pocket.

"Nothing came through for him yet. So he's still acting major."

"Damn," he mumbled. "If anyone deserves promotion, it's Ellis."

Tom pulled another paper out of his coat pocket and handed it to Lawrence, then took a small New Testament out of the same pocket. "Before we lose the light altogether, we got to make you official. Put your hand on the Bible and read the oath of office. Dr. Townsend and John will be the witnesses."

He took the paper and looked at it, glad to see someone had taken the time to print it in large letters, going over them so they were dark.

"I did the printing. Did it large 'cause I didn't think you had your glasses with you," John confessed.

He smiled, put his right hand on the small Bible, held the paper at a comfortable distance in his left and read out loud, "I, Joshua Lawrence Chamberlain, do solemnly swear that I have never voluntarily borne arms against the United States since I have been a citizen thereof; that I have voluntarily given no aid, countenance, counsel, or encouragement to persons engaged in armed hostility thereto. And I do further swear that to the best of my knowledge and ability, I will support and defend the Constitution of the United States against all enemies, foreign or domestic, that I will bear true and faithful allegiance to the same; that I take this obligation freely, without any mental reservation or purpose of evasion, and that I will well and truthfully discharge the duties of the office on which I am about to enter, so help me God."

The light of day was gone by the time he finished. Just visible between the clouds, a near full moon had begun to rise over the trees. Tom took the Bible away and put it in his coat pocket, pulling out new shoulder straps with the silver eagles of a colonel on them. "Oh, before I forget. These are yours, too. Maybe you can get Mrs.

Donaldson to sew them on your coat so you are all nice and official when you get back to us tomorrow."

"Congratulations, Colonel," Dr. Townsend said and shook his hand.

"Thank you, Doctor," he said as he took the shoulder straps from his brother.

"Well, we better be getting back to camp before we are listed as AWOL," Dr. Townsend said, mounting his horse.

"John and I will be by tomorrow morning first thing to escort you back. We're bivouacked about three miles down the road in a big field," Tom said. "See you then."

"See you tomorrow," he returned.

The group turned their horses and rode down the farm lane at a brisk trot for the road. He stood there a moment alone in the moonlight, the new shoulder straps in hand, the embroidered silver eagles framed by gold bullion feeling rough against his fingers. They were visible evidence that his new rank was official, a goal he had been striving for since last summer.

The responsibility they represented loomed greater than ever, almost daunting. He would have difficult on the spot decisions to make in the coming combat, what risks to take in obeying orders from the generals. He would have to accept the embarrassment and danger of being wrong and making mistakes on the battlefield. All his shortcomings were staring him in the face. He was not West Point. He had no real experience as a commander in combat, only book learning and what Ames had taught him. He could not count the experience at Fredericksburg as combat. It was not a stand-up fight with maneuvers he had to think through and order, but it had been more an advance and holding action. He was well aware, too, that he was not fully recovered from the sunstroke and thus, he was impaired. He could only hope he would be worthy of the silver eagles, be as cool and commanding as Ames when the real test came.

That test looked as if it was going to be on Union soil this time, and he knew it would be a fight they could not afford to lose. He stood watching the riders disappear down the empty, dark road. The cool damp night breeze chilled him, and he shivered. He turned and walked up the porch stairs and into the house, closing the door behind him. He left the shoulder straps on the small table by the clothes rack where his coat hung and climbed the stairs, feeling this might be the last good night's sleep in a real bed he'd have for a while.

* * *

He awoke before dawn to the irresistible scents of bacon and eggs cooking. The humidity and aftereffects of the fever left him still feeling washed out, but today was not the day to give into it. He quickly got dressed and came downstairs to get his coat off the clothes rack by the door. He planned to ask Mrs. Donaldson if she would sew on the new shoulder straps and intended to pay her for the work. When he reached the bottom of the stairs and looked, he discovered the coat was missing.

Mr. Donaldson, lean and wiry with a full white beard, came out of the dining room to his left. "Come to breakfast, Colonel. My missus has cooked up every egg in the danged hen house. And some good lean bacon and biscuits, too."

"Thank you, sir," he said and followed the old man into the dining room. Mrs. Donaldson, a tiny sprite of a woman, came out of the small kitchen with a heaping plate of scrambled eggs. She put them next to a platter of bacon and basket of biscuits in the center of an oak table covered with a red checkered tablecloth set with modest china. On the back of one of the chairs was his coat with the new silver eagles. He stood at the door, surprised.

"Well, it's the least I could do, Colonel, you comin' with the army and chasing those Rebels out of Maryland, keepin' them away

137

from our chickens and hogs. You need a good hardy breakfast, too, to get your strength back." She smiled. "Now sit down and help yourself while it's hot. I'll go get the coffee. I'll want to thank your brothers for it again."

He sat and found Mr. Donaldson helping himself to a good portion of the eggs. The old man passed him the plate.

"Eat up, Colonel. Your fever's past. No sense starving yourself."

Mrs. Donaldson came in with the coffee and filled the cups, then sat at her place.

"Thank you," Lawrence said, taking some eggs. He passed the plate to her. They ate in silence, having talked themselves out the night before. There was something somber in the quiet meal.

Finally, Mr. Donaldson asked, "Think there's going to be a big battle, Colonel?"

"Yes, I believe so, sir," he said. "Lee is a big threat to Washington and Pennsylvania."

"Well, you be careful, Colonel. Don't leave your wife a widow, like what happened to our daughter, Emily," Mrs. Donaldson said, looking at him with sad eyes.

"I'll do what I can, but I learned a long time ago to put my life in the hands of Providence," he said. "So far the Lord has kept me from harm in battle."

After breakfast when his brothers failed to arrive, he went out to the barn and saddled the chestnut gelding. As he led the horse out into a misting drizzle of rain, he found the Donaldsons on the porch and walked the horse over to them.

"Wanted to see you off before we continue with our chores," Mr. Donaldson said. "Take care, son."

"Thank you for your hospitality," he said.

"Thank you for the coffee. You'll always be welcome at our house. And you and the boys will be in our prayers," Mrs. Donaldson called.

"Wish I was thirty years younger. I'd come with you myself," Mr. Donaldson said. "I'd help you whip them Rebs."

"Oh, Papa," Mrs. Donaldson said and wrapped her arms around her husband's shoulders in a hug. "Don't be such a foolish old man."

He mounted the gelding, smiled and waved at them, then headed down the lane through the wheat field toward the road.

"Whip 'em good, Colonel," the old man called after him.

When he reached the road, he turned right and set out at a walk. Checking his pocket watch, he found it was five past seven. He figured the army had a good head start on him and hoped he'd run into his brothers soon. The sky promised more than a drizzle, maybe a deluge any moment. It was too hot and humid to bother with the poncho. He rode on, looking to the right at the land, marveling at the Donaldson's vast field of wheat. He thought with envy how lucky the farmers were in Virginia and Maryland. They had rich level land. Maine farmland was mostly hills and rocks, and it took exhaustive effort to make it yield crops. Flat fields that went on for acres were a luxury back home. He remembered how he and his brothers in their younger years struggled to clear the family's hilly farm fields of rocks that seemed to reappear like a demon crop every spring, heaved up by winter freezing.

He put the gelding into an easy canter along the firmer ground on the side of the road, trying to make some time, wondering where his brothers were. The army was easy to follow, having left the muddy road full of thousands of overlapping tracks and wheel ruts.

After going about three miles, he slowed the gelding to a trot, then a walk as he approached a trampled field with burned-out campfires that told of a bivouac. He pushed on at a slow canter, figuring if he kept up a fast pace, he'd soon catch the army. After all, a single man on a horse could travel faster than thousands of men slogging along in the mud. He followed the trampled road, alternating between a slow canter and a walk to rest the horse and himself.

139

After two hours, he started to pass stragglers with sore feet and worn-out bodies sitting on the side of the road. Most ignored him cantering past, too caught up in their own misery. One flagged him down. He saw the red Maltese cross on the cap. As he drew closer, he recognized the young man as Burk, one of his students who had joined.

"Colonel Chamberlain," Burk called out, looking quite pale.

He rode over and reined in the horse by the boy.

"Lord, am I glad to see you're back," he panted.

"What happened to you?" Lawrence asked.

"Ate something that didn't agree with me, sir. Been puking my guts out since before we left at 4:30. Think the worst is over now. Wanted you to know I'll catch up as soon as I can." He held up a slip of paper. "See, Major Spear gave me this permission ticket to keep handy, since our company commander, Lieutenant Lewis, is still under arrest from getting back late from leave. You go on, sir. I'll see you later."

"Have you seen Tom or John?"

"Not since early this morning, sir. They were at the head of the regiment with the major. They didn't pass me going the other way. I've been keeping my eyes on the road for Rebel cavalry. Rumor says they're around these parts. Watch yourself, sir."

"I will. Don't push yourself too hard. Take a drink of water when your stomach settles."

Burk nodded.

Lawrence put the gelding into a slow canter and continued down the road. Early in the afternoon, he rode into Middleburg, Maryland, finding the town bustling with everyday activity and a few soldiers loitering about, nursing sore feet or filling canteens at various water pumps by public horse troughs. In a drizzling rain, he reached a swift running creek on the other side of town. The gelding plunged in and splashed across where the army had gone before.

140

He had traveled about another five miles when he spotted movement ahead. The rain stopped and with it the gray haze. The movement became soldiers, not stragglers, but soldiers moving with rifles at the ready, led by a few mounted officers. He had found the rear guard of the Corps. He slowed the gelding.

Coming toward him from far up the line, he noticed a familiar gray horse and knew John was the rider. A mounted officer suddenly rode across John's path and stopped him. John took a crumpled paper out of his jacket and showed it to the officer, looked up in his direction, waved wildly, and pointed at him. The officer turned in his saddle and watched him as he approached. Riding closer, he noticed the officer was a captain. The captain saluted. He returned it.

"Sir, I am Captain Talbot of the 9th Massachusetts. This man claims to be your brother. Are you Colonel Chamberlain of the 20th Maine?" Talbot asked.

"Yes, Captain Talbot, I am, and he is my brother John. He is a member of the Christian Commission visiting the regiment to assist our hospital steward. We have no surgeon," he explained.

"Fine, sir. That corresponds to what he just told me. We can't be too careful at this point. There have been signs of enemy cavalry in the area. We don't want any spies getting through."

"Spy? I'm not ..." John protested, but fell silent at a sharp look from his brother.

"I understand, Captain. I'll take it from here," Lawrence said.

"Yes, sir." Talbot saluted and he returned it. Then Talbot rode toward the rear guard.

"John, what's going on? I expected you at the farm first thing in the morning." He pulled the gelding next to Prince, and the brothers rode past the rear guard at a slow trot.

"Well, the army had other ideas," John explained. "Meade wants the whole army to pick up the pace and get itself into the lightest possible marching order. The order came to Ellis last night

141

that all commanders are to send away excess wagons, baggage, and animals. The damned bugle sounded reveille before daylight, and we were on the road at 4:30. We could encounter the enemy at any moment, Ellis said. Didn't think it was safe for me to wander and didn't want to send Tom with me because he might need him. Besides, the 20th Maine ended up at the very head of the column on point today."

"Oh."

"It gets better. We got through Middleburg around noon, and as soon as we crossed Big Pipe Creek, there were signs of Confederate cavalry. Someone saw a dead horse and a lot of tracks. Ellis sent out a company on both sides to act as skirmishers, and that slowed the whole column to a crawl. The 44th New York just took over the skirmish line, and Ellis figured it was safe to let me go look for you. He wrote me out this permission slip so I wouldn't get picked up as a spy. I've been stopped four times already. You'd think they'd figure out that if a civilian is riding with the army that he belongs there in some capacity."

"John, everyone's worked up at this point, so anything can happen. You haven't been in a combat situation, so you wouldn't know how crazy things can get with rumors flying and conflicting reports. But you're with me now and won't be stopped again."

"Well, I'm sure glad you're back. Ellis will be, too. He's still ill and about beat. Most of the boys are about beat. At least a third of the regiment ends up straggling every day."

"That always happens on a hard march, John. It's all new to you, I know."

They fell silent and rode along past the troops. Lawrence noticed the men had all become ragged. Muddy and footsore, some were marching in their stocking feet, while others were barefoot, their shoes hanging on their bayonets or tucked in blanket rolls. Many were so hot and uncomfortable, they were marching in their drawers, with colorful bandannas tied about their heads or necks to soak up sweat, their uniforms rolled up in blanket rolls. They presented anything but a military appearance marching down the muddy road. He and John passed regiment after regiment riding toward the head of the column.

At last he spotted Company K in the rear of his regiment with the dashing young Lieutenant James Nichols in command. Nichols must have heard their horses approaching, for he suddenly turned to look back at them.

Recognition showed on his face, and as they passed he yelled, "Colonel Chamberlain's back!"

They rode toward the color guard at the front of the column where Tom and Ellis were riding along slowly, almost in a daze. The regiment began to perk up. Cheering and whistles followed them. Ellis turned in his saddle, then Tom. Both officers' faces brightened.

"God, you're a sight for sore eyes!" Ellis burst out. "Was afraid we were going into a major fight without you."

"You look a lot better, Colonel," Tom added. "How you feelin'?"

"I'll make it," he said and smiled. He noticed Ellis still looked pale. "How are you doing, Ellis?"

"Tolerable … barely. But I'll make it, too." He forced a smile. "We've got to make up for that slacker, Gilmore."

Lawrence looked back at the regiment, finding it considerably smaller than he had left it. "Looks like we lost quite a few to straggling."

"It's the damned weather and forced marching," Ellis grumbled. "If the dust and heat don't get you, the humidity and rain do."

"Ain't that the truth," Tom added.

"Well, you're back and that's what counts," Ellis said. "Takes the pressure off me."

"You did fine, Ellis. You did fine," he said.

They fell silent, watching the New York skirmishers out ahead in the lengthening shadows. A town appeared on the road ahead, Union Mills by the sign. He looked at his pocket watch. It was 6 o'clock. As they approached the town, the civilians came out of their shops and homes, waving and cheering.

A man in oversized clothes shouted, "The rebel cavalry went through here not seven hours ago. Took everything they could carry."

He saw people on the roadside selling food at reasonable prices. A woman, who had to be seventy years old, approached him from the side of the road, struggling over uneven ground with her cane. He pulled the gelding to a stop.

"Got to tell you," she called. "They got cavalry, sir. They got cavalry and two artilleries and are right smart of men with guns!"

"Yes, ma'am. Thank you for the information. We'll find them," he said, touching the visor of his cap. "You just be careful now, and don't come out on this muddy road. We'll see to them."

She nodded, smiled, and carefully picked her way back to firmer ground.

The brigade bivouacked outside of Union Mills in a large fallow field in the deepening twilight. As the troops settled in, he began to hear artillery firing off toward the north beyond the Maryland border. He abruptly came to the full realization that Lee had truly moved his invasion all the way into northern territory, and the men would soon be fighting the first major battle on their own soil.

Sitting on the trunk of a fallen tree and drinking some coffee, he stared out into the dark trees at the edge of the field, watching fireflies. There seemed to be something hanging in the air besides humidity—a heavy tension of an unknown future, a future that would be cut short by a bullet for many he now watched moving in the twilight around him if they saw action this time. The responsibility represented by the silver eagles on his shoulder straps suddenly weighed heavier than ever on him. The same worry that plagued Ames in the beginning now began to prey on his mind. *Were they ready? Let it go. Leave it in God's hands.* But for some uncomfortable reason, that was becoming very difficult.

At 7:00 in the morning on the first day of July, they marched away from Union Mills with the rest of the 5th Corps under intermittent rain. Ellis rode next to him at the head of the regiment. The acting major was still plagued by diarrhea, looked pale, and was not smoking his pipe due to the rain.

"This is ridiculous. We don't know what the positions are or the movements of the other corps of this army. We only know that Lee is somewhere in Pennsylvania. How the hell can the top brass run a campaign this way? For all we know, Harrisburg or Philadelphia could be under attack," Ellis griped.

"Ellis, relax. I suspect they'll tell us what we need to know when we need to know it," Lawrence said.

"Can't believe you have that much faith in this army and those running it, the way things have been going."

"I do have faith in God and that things will be revealed in their own time, Ellis."

"Well, I still feel we're liable to run into a world of hurt without much warning before this day is out, Colonel."

"It would not come as a surprise to me at this point. But just as at Fredericksburg, all we can do is be ready and take things as they come."

The troops ahead of them suddenly slowed in their march. Colonel Rice came into view, trotting his horse toward them from up the line.

"I bet that's trouble coming right now," Ellis said.

Rice pulled in next to him and smiled pleasantly, putting him at ease. "Gentlemen. Colonel, it is good to see you back. Just got word you returned."

"Thank you. Do you know why our progress has slowed?"

"Signs of the enemy ahead. A broken caisson and a dead Rebel cavalryman with indications that many horses have passed. Skirmishers were sent out. You know how that always slows things up. Might run into the Rebels any time now."

"See, I knew it," Ellis said.

"I better get back to my boys. It's good to see you." He swung his horse around and cantered back up the line toward the 44th New York.

With every slow, quiet mile the tension grew. Lawrence found himself staring into every patch of woods and up at every ridge line of a hill wondering if the enemy would suddenly appear or begin shelling them. A nagging doubt reached out from the recesses of his mind again. *Are you ready to command in a combat situation?* He shook his head. *Stop it. You think too much.*

The rain finally stopped and the sky brightened some, and so did his mood. They passed a stone monument that marked the border of Pennsylvania. He took out his pocket watch. It was noon. He turned in his saddle, looked back at his regiment and shouted, "Welcome to Pennsylvania!"

Drums began to beat and a band began to play "Yankee Doodle" in the 83rd Pennsylvania up ahead, now back on its native soil. A new enthusiasm raced along the line like an electric current, perking up tired men. He looked back, saw Sergeant Tozier unfurl the colors and smile up at him.

"Can't let them outdo us, sir."

Their own musicians struck up "Yankee Doodle," and the regiment took up the regular marching step without being ordered. The land began to change around them. Broad fertile fields of wheat and corn were interspersed with orchards. The trees hung heavy with ripening cherries, apples, and peaches. It was all very tempting. Huge stone barns and neat white farmhouses were seen here and there. The only thing strange about the pastoral scene was that no livestock was in evidence. *The farmers probably took their stock away to hide from the armies.*

They passed roadside stands set up by local Pennsylvania Dutch inhabitants, who were busy selling milk, buttermilk, bread, cake, and pies at inflated prices. Among these civilians were several strapping young fellows, who looked as if they should be carrying a rifle in service of their country.

He heard young Lewis, another student of his in the color company behind him yell, "You ought to be with us fighting to protect your land and loved ones."

One of the young men glared as if insulted, puffed out his chest, and shot back in a German-accented voice, "No, English, you fights for me. That is why I pays my taxes!"

"Why mud, blood, and shee-yut!" Lewis yelled. "Boys, let's buy his whole stock and charge it to Uncle Sam!"

Lawrence turned in his saddle in time to see Lewis and half the company break ranks and swarm the stand like locusts. He did nothing to stop it, could not abide the self-serving attitude of the young Dutchman.

"You're no better than them Rebels!" the Dutchman protested.

The sun came out as the afternoon wore on. In spite of the heat, he felt a chill as he rode. An unshakable sense of foreboding hung in the air like thick morning mist.

Nearing Hanover, they came upon more signs of war: dead horses and corpses of Rebel cavalrymen. *This must have been the source of the artillery I heard last night.* They reached Hanover by midafternoon. The people came out into the street to greet them with enthusiastic cheers. On a balcony, a group of young ladies dressed in red, white, and blue appeared and sang "The Star-Spangled

Banner." Others handed out glasses of cold well water or milk and fresh bread.

Outside of town, a halt was called, for which he was thankful. The men could not push on further without rest. He felt lightheaded and knew the fever had come back. He slid off the horse and barely kept his knees from buckling under him. He just stood, watching the regiment while feeling came back to his legs, one hand holding onto the saddle to steady himself, hoping no one would notice.

John rode over to him. "You all right, Lawrence?"

"It's been a hard day. I'll be all right with a little rest and something to eat," he said and forced a smile.

"I don't know. I think you're pushing yourself too hard."

He decided to change the subject, fast. "Where've you been?"

"Helping some of the boys who petered out along the side of the road. Talked to Colonel Rice and Dr. Townsend on the way. I'll see you later, maybe. Dr. Townsend is going to show me how to bandage correctly and tie a tourniquet while he has the chance. Then I'll be of more help when we have to set up an aid station. You make sure you get something to eat and drink. I don't want to see you pass out like that ever again."

"I will, John. I will."

John nodded and headed for the 44th New York.

Lawrence watched the men stack their rifles. Some scattered in every direction to search for water and fence rails for fires. A few forage wagons pulled up with food from local farms, and men rushed the tailgates to get their share. Fires were started and cooking began.

Listening to the distant thunder of artillery, he sat on a log under a massive oak tree, finishing a chicken leg. There was too much artillery fire to be a minor skirmish. It sounded more like a major battle off to the west. Tom walked over with Captain Joseph Fitch of Company D.

"Sir, we got a problem," Tom said.

148

"What?" he asked and tossed the bone away. He did not feel like dealing with any problems right now. He just wanted to rest.

"Sir, three men from the old 2nd Maine that were being held under guard in my company got away." Fitch said. "I don't know exactly when, but I reckon it was someplace between the border and here. They're probably on their way to Maine by now."

"Damn," he muttered. "Who?"

"Benjamin West, Samuel Morrison, and James Kelley. Only stupid thing Morrison has done over two years. The other two haven't even been in a year yet. Had no right to protest their lot. Haven't been in long enough."

"Well, we can't do anything about it now. I'm certainly not going to start a search for them," Lawrence said. "That leaves us with only a handful still under arrest. Tom, record the names of the deserters. We'll make a formal report when our regimental papers catch up with us again, whenever that will be. Both of you go get something to eat. I have a feeling we won't be staying here the night. Not with the sound of so much artillery to the west."

Tom and Fitch left. Tom returned with a plate full of chicken and two tin cups of hot coffee. Tom sat down on the log and passed the plate to him. He took a breast, then one of the cups.

"Got some news," Tom said. "It ain't good, but it's just a bunch of rumors at present."

"Don't keep me in suspense," he said and took a swallow of coffee, feeling it send a warm and refreshing glow coursing through his tired, feverish body. He knew better than to believe rumors, but sometimes there was a grain of truth in them.

"Well, from what I heard, the army ran into Lee at some little town west of here called Gettysburg. The 1st and 11th Corps were hit hard and have barely held on against overwhelming numbers. General John Reynolds, one of our best commanders, has been shot dead."

149

He thought briefly of Ames with the 11th. "Given the lack of real information over the last few days and the way we've been groping blindly through the Pennsylvania countryside, Tom, I'd take that all with a very large grain of salt."

"That's what I say but figured you'd want to know." They fell silent and ate what remained of the chicken.

Lawrence had just finished the last of his coffee when a staff officer came riding through their camp on a sweaty, wild-eyed horse. The officer stopped by Captain Land. He heard Land's voice boom out as he pointed, "The Colonel? Over there by that oak."

The staff officer rode over, stopped the horse, and saluted. Lawrence quickly stood and returned it, feeling the chicken turn to a lump in his gut. This was it. It had to be.

"Sir, I've come from Colonel Vincent. He sends his compliments. Prepare to move out. The 1st and 11th Corps ran into Lee at a town called Gettysburg about fifteen miles from here. They've been hit hard and were driven back through Gettysburg. They are now dug in on some hills on the south side of town, waiting for the rest of the army. General Reynolds is dead. We'll be marching through the night, sir."

"Damn, it is true," Tom blurted, standing.

"We'll be ready," Lawrence said. The officer nodded, pulled his horse around, and rode to the next regiment with the dismal news.

"Tom, get Ellis. Tell him to get the men up and assembled." Watching Tom run off, he could not help wondering if Ames was all right. Knowing the general, he'd be right in the middle of it, cool as ice on his big bay horse.

The regiment got itself together in the twilight shadows. Cicadas still called in the darkening trees. The cool of evening had not yet arrived. Soon bugles all down the lines were sounding "Forward!" and they were pushing westward again.

Sergeant Tozier and the color guard insisted on keeping the colors flying to let all they passed know what manner of men were coming to redeem the day for the Union. He was glad to let the sergeant have his way and rode at the head of the column with his brothers and Ellis, all in a silent, contemplative mood, with Ellis back to smoking his pipe. A full moon rose in midevening, casting a clear blue light over the countryside almost as bright as day. Fireflies flashed in the grass and brush and flitted along the edge of the road, giving the evening an air of enchantment. They rode in a dreamy silence but for the jingle and clank of equipment, taken in by the spell of the night.

Lawrence began to think of his children, six-year-old Daisy and four-year-old Wyllys, chasing fireflies in the front yard last July. He placed the captives in a Mason jar covered in cheesecloth so the children could get a close look. He let them go after the children went to bed and remembered how Fannie teased him, telling him they were *only* insects.

Suddenly, Colonel Vincent and his staff rode up from behind, startling him out of his reverie. There was a civilian with them, a middle-aged man with a beard, wearing a broad-brimmed straw hat and duster.

"It is good to see you up and well, Colonel," Vincent said pulling his horse alongside.

"Thank you, sir."

"Let me introduce Mr. Charles Coffin, a reporter from the *Boston Journal*. He has been riding with the army since the beginning of June. Mr. Coffin, this is Colonel Joshua Lawrence Chamberlain, my newest regimental commander."

"Colonel, my pleasure," Coffin said with a polite nod.

"Mr. Coffin," Lawrence said, not so sure he liked the idea of having a reporter riding along. He had not forgotten the trouble the press caused him a year ago by exposing his plans to join the army instead of going on the planned sabbatical to Europe.

151

"Colonel Chamberlain, mind if I ask your opinion of the war being brought into our own backyard?" Coffin asked.

"No, not at all. When the fight starts, it is one we had better win. Meade is a good and practical soldier. As you know, he was in command of our 5th Corps until his promotion. I think he can do it. The regiments are certainly ready and in no mood for another defeat." He did not feel up to a more involved answer.

Vincent looked up at their colors flying in the gentle night breeze. Caught up in the moment, he took off his cap. "What death more glorious could any man desire than to die on this soil of old Pennsylvania, fighting for that flag?"

"Much prefer the Rebs die on this soil for invading Pennsylvania, Colonel, sir," Tozier spoke up behind them from the color guard.

"I tend to agree with the color sergeant, Colonel Vincent," Ellis added.

"Pay no mind, sir," Lawrence said, the thought of losing Vincent chilling him. He prayed it was not some strange portent that prompted Vincent to make such a statement. "Yours is a fine patriotic sentiment. But I prefer you alive as we all do."

As they rounded a bend in the road, a staff officer rode up and whispered to Vincent. His face seemed to brighten in the moonlight. "Gentlemen, I have an announcement from General Barnes, our division commander," he said in a loud voice. "McClellan is at the head of the army in Gettysburg!"

The 83rd Pennsylvania ahead of them burst into explosive cheers that ran up and down the line like the roar of an ocean wave. Lawrence was not sure if it was true or not. Vincent waved his cap and yelled, "Now, boys, we'll give 'em hell tomorrow." The colonel put his cap back on and turned to him. "Colonel Chamberlain, stay well. I'll be needing you and all my field officers tomorrow."

152

Then he rode on ahead toward the front of the brigade, with his staff and Mr. Coffin trailing. The ethereal mood of the moonlight on the rolling Pennsylvania countryside became intoxicating.

"Hey, Andrew," Lawrence heard from the Color Company behind them, calling the sergeant. "Did you hear some fellow saw General George Washington's spirit on a white horse riding over the hills?"

"On this night with the country in peril, I wouldn't be surprised," Tozier shouted back.

The powers of the other world seemed to be so near on such a night that Lawrence half believed it himself as he gazed out on the moon-silvered country around him. To speed the 5th Corps along, it was ordered that the units divide up and head to Gettysburg on separate roads to prevent the clogging up of any one route. A sense of deep urgency gripped him in spite of his growing fatigue.

They passed through McSherrystown and Bonnaughtown before turning south off the Hanover Road, and they marched through the night until they reached the Baltimore Pike below Rock Creek. Here they halted.

He checked his pocket watch, found it was after midnight, and knew they had covered more than thirty miles since sunrise. Hardly able to move, he dismounted stiffly. Thomas saw to the horse while he spread his blanket under a maple tree and removed his sword belt. He sat on the blanket a minute, his knees feeling like jelly and his leg muscles shaking with fatigue. Then he eased down on the ground, suddenly finding it hard and uncomfortable, though it had been fine last night. *Maybe it was just the tension of the coming fight, or maybe I had been spoiled from sleeping in a bed.* Using his cap for a pillow, he settled down. He dropped off to sleep almost as soon as he closed his eyes, the low noise of the camp and the aches in his muscles fading away.

He was awake before sunrise and walked through the camp where others were just stirring. The sticky humidity made him feel uncomfortable. He opened the first three buttons of his coat and the first two on his sweat-stained white shirt. He was glad to see the regiment had grown some in numbers with soldiers who wandered in during the night. Reveille blew, and the men managed a hasty breakfast before it was time to fall in. He knew that for many this would be their last march, their last few hours of life … maybe his own last few hours of life. His heart thumped. *No, don't think it. Not now.*

He was finishing the last of the coffee Thomas had brought him and watching the regiment assemble when Tom walked over and handed him a paper. "Courier brought this. Orders, sir, from General Meade. All regimental commanders are to read this to their men before we head out," Tom said. Lawrence handed Tom the empty cup and took the paper.

He skimmed it quickly as he walked toward the center of the assembled column. They were in for a serious fight. He was sure, now, without question. He stopped and cleared his throat. "Men, your attention, please. This is General Meade's first order to the Army of the Potomac." His voice carried across the regiment.

"Oh, Lord, here we go again," someone said in the line.

"Old Snapping Turtle's got to justify his new position," another voice sounded further down.

Lawrence ignored the sneering jests of the jaded soldiers. Most of them were giving him their full attention. He went on. "Headquarters Army of The Potomac, June 30, 1863. The commanding general requests that previous to the engagement soon expected with the enemy, corps and all other commanding officers will address their troops, explaining to them the immense issues involved in this struggle. The enemy is on our soil. The whole country now looks anxiously to this army to deliver it from the presence of the foe. Our failure to do so will leave us no such

154

welcome as the swelling of millions of hearts with pride and joy as our success would give to every soldier in the army. The Army has fought well heretofore; it is believed that it will fight more desperately and bravely than ever if it is addressed in fitting terms." He paused and cleared his throat. "Corps and other commanders are authorized to order the instant death of any soldier who fails in his duty at this hour. By command of Major General Meade, Commander, Army of the Potomac."

There was a stunned silence, punctuated only by a few coughs and the rattle of equipment as men shifted on their feet. All felt the gravity of the situation. It was etched on their sun-bronzed faces. If they lost this one, it was highly possible they would lose the war, and everyone was expected to do his part to prevent that. Then the somber spell was broken.

Captain Land's voice boomed from Company H. "Well, boys, you know what this means. If you don't get out there and get shot, you're going to be shot by me or one of the other officers. Not that some of you don't deserve it ... like I've been threatening you for months." Nervous laughter ran through the ranks. Lawrence knew Land liked to crack jokes to boost the spirit of the men and would probably keep it up until the bullets started flying.

"Captain Land, I want you and the other officers to inspect the weapons now. We don't want any last-minute problems," he called.

"Yes, sir," Land yelled back. The officers moved quickly among the men of their companies before it was time to move out.

Under a red sun in the stifling humid July heat, they marched the remaining few miles toward Gettysburg, reaching the hills on the south end of town before noon. At first, the division halted south of Wolf's Hill next to the 12th Corps. Then the entire division crossed over Rock Creek, stopping at the crossroads near the McAllister's Mill, and finally took up a reserve position in a peach orchard.

Lawrence had the men stack arms. They rested, cooked coffee, wrote a last-minute letter home, or spoke in quiet, subdued undertones as if in church. The sounds of battle grew in front of them beyond the hills.

He stood beside the gelding, taking swallows from the canteen. He looked toward the hills. White puffs of exploding shells appeared above them. Close. It was very close.

He strapped the canteen to the saddle and looked around. He saw the 20th was nestled between other regiments in the 5th Corps along a road. Beyond and around them, he could just make out the flags of the 1st, 11th, and 12th Corps. Too aware of his own shortcomings as a military commander, Lawrence began to worry again.

More than anything, he was impressed by the great calm, the uncertainty of a beginning, the seeming lack of a tactical plan for a battle. Nothing was as he had imagined. No meetings or discussions over maps. He was too far below those who made the decisions. Everything on the regimental level boiled down to waiting. He was acutely aware of other troops coming up on either side of him, but he had no idea how they would be used.

He couldn't guess where the battle would begin in this part of the field. He wondered if the other more experienced officers in the regiments around him were bothered by all this uncertainty. *Maybe it was only the generals who really knew what was going on*. Then one order came down—to hold his men ready to take part in action on the army's right. He mounted the gelding. Shortly after the order came through, an ordnance wagon showed up. The men drew twenty extra rounds of ammunition, stuffing them in their pockets or adding them to the forty rounds already in their cartridge boxes. *Things should speed up now*. He felt his heart beat harder and a drop of sweat trickle down his back.

His attention was drawn to a noisy fight for a small wooded hill on their right front. Someone said the locals called it Culp's Hill after a family that owned the ground. He was sure they would be sent toward it at any moment. He found himself looking up and

156

down the column for a mounted courier who would bring the orders. Artillery opened up behind them and to the left, accompanied by the familiar rattle of muskets. Bugles sounded. The 1st Division of the 5th Corps, with the 3rd Brigade up front, pushed to the left. The men were suddenly off the road, marching through a swamp, scrambling over stone walls and through hedges while the earth shook as they moved toward the exploding shells. His gelding, with little urging, flew over the walls and hedges as if he had wings, showing no fear of the noise.

Disturbing news filtered down the line to him. They were rushing to support General Daniel Sickels's 3rd Corps, but it was not where it was supposed to be. Instead, it was a mile forward, desperately trying to hold off Confederate troops hitting its front and flank. After crossing a road, the 1st Division halted on the edge of a wheat field. Lawrence sat on the gelding awaiting orders, wondering why they had stopped the advance. Ellis rode up. "What's going on, sir?" Ellis asked with an impatient edge to his voice.

"Ellis, I haven't a clue and am tired of being left in the dark."

"You and me both, sir." They fell silent, watching the 1st and 2nd Brigade of their division on their right suddenly break off and move into a wooded area beyond the wheat field where they immediately joined the battle.

His heart began to race and his breath came short. Would they be next? To the left, the far end of the 3rd Corps fought desperately near a boulder-strewn corner of the valley. Some of the huge rocks were the size of a Maine barn.

A bugle blew. Suddenly, the brigade was forming a battle line on the edge of the wheat field. Orders were passed. When the maneuvers were completed, the 20th Maine ended up positioned between the 16th Michigan and the 83rd Pennsylvania on their left, and the 44th New York on its right. Lawrence sat his horse out in front by the colors. Colonel Vincent rode past and kept going, trailed by his staff and a mounted orderly carrying the brigade flag. Mr. Coffin was still with him.

With a regiment on either side of him in an open field and Vincent in sight, his anxiety began to melt. He saw he had good support, and any fighting would be where he could see every move and have plenty of time to react. He realized he could not have asked for a better position in the brigade line. Firing directly ahead drew his gaze to the far end of the wheat field. He could see blue-clad troops falling back through waist-high wheat. From somewhere behind him, a battery began firing, lobbing shells into the smoky woods beyond the wheat field. Vincent came riding back and pulled in his horse next to Colonel Rice. They talked for a few moments, Vincent pointing to the left behind them. Curious, Lawrence turned in his saddle to see what his brigade commander was pointing at.

It was a bald-faced hill on the extreme left of the Union line. The slope was strewn with rocks and boulders that seemed to compete with bushes, scrub oak, and pine for space. Beyond it loomed a larger hill, covered from top to bottom with a thick forest of trees. These two hills dominated the land.

He thought he saw movement on the smaller one. When Vincent and his staff rode straight at the hills as if the devil himself was chasing them, he realized that whoever took those hills held the key to the whole field. When he turned his attention to his right, he saw Rice riding straight at him. The colonel hauled his horse to a skidding stop. "Follow the 44th. We're heading for the summit of the little rocky hill," Rice shouted above the shooting to their front. "General Warren wants troops up there, and we're it."

Then he rode on to the 16th Michigan with the order. Tom was suddenly alongside.

"Where we going?"

"That hill," Lawrence said, pointing. "Where's John? Haven't seen him in a while."

"He went up that same hill with General Howard's brother, Rowland, to have a look at the area. Said he'd find us. Was just coming to tell you. We'll probably run into him."

The 3rd Brigade marched out, following a narrow farm lane and crossing a creek over a crude log bridge. As they neared the north end of the smaller hill, they circled behind it. They followed an old lumber trail up the east slope in the lengthening shadows of late afternoon. The rays of the lowering sun turned patches of forest to green fire.

Enemy artillery opened up. Shells exploded overhead, sending tree limbs down on the column as well as deadly shell and rock fragments. John came riding up to Lawrence and Tom at the head of the regiment. John shook hands with them. "Guess you're going in. I want to wish you ..."

Before he could finish his words, a shell flew past so close they felt the compressed air. It hit nearby with an ear-shattering explosion.

Lawrence looked at his brothers. "Boys," he said, "I don't like this. Another such shot might make it hard for Mother. John, ride on ahead and prepare a place for our wounded. Tom, go back and make sure the line is well closed up."

The two brothers left on their separate missions.

Behind him, he heard Chaplain Luther French say, "Lord, Captain Clark, did you see that? The shell slammed into that officer's horse and ..."

Captain Atherton Clark retorted, "For Christ's sake, Chaplain, if you have business, attend to it!"

Lawrence looked over his shoulder and saw the crestfallen chaplain heading toward him. He pulled the gelding to a stop off the trail, out of the way of the regiment. "Chaplain French, please assist John and Hospital Steward Baker in setting up the aid station for the men. I expect we will have need of it very soon. I'll assign the drummer boys and other noncombatants to be stretcher bearers."

"Yes, Colonel," French said and dashed off after John.

The shelling forced the column to move below the crest of the hill. More branches and tree limbs showered down on them. In the brutal July heat, exhaustion was still taking its toll. He saw some of the men who gave out scramble for cover in the rocks while others who had been following as stragglers finally caught up.

Among the returning latecomers he spotted Burk. The reality that a fight was very near pushed through the feverish fog that threatened to cloud his thinking and reactions. As soon as Ellis rode up to him, he turned to the acting major and said, "Ellis, release the Pioneers and provost guard to their companies. Detail the drummer boys as stretcher-bearers, and allow the cooks and servants, at their own request, to take up rifles. The rest can fill in and help the wounded get back to the aid station. I think we'll be needing every man we've got in this fight."

"Yes, sir," Ellis said and rode away.

Riding down the line he came to the seven 2nd Maine holdouts sitting in a small group, sullen and frowning. "We need every man in the line," Lawrence said with cold frankness. "This may very well be the last battle. If any of you would care to join us, I would appreciate it."

"Oh, hell, I'm not going to sit here and get shot at without shooting back," one young man said and stood up. "I'm with you, Colonel." He turned to his companions. "Any of you want to join me?" Three stood up.

"Go see Major Spear about rifles. As to you three, I'll expect you to be here when this is over. I can't spare anyone to guard you."

They avoided his stare. Not wanting to spend any more precious time on them, he rode on down the line. He found Vincent dismounted on the southern end of the hill sending the 44th with Rice to start the line of battle. Mr. Coffin was off to one side writing furiously on a sheaf of papers in his hand.

Seeing the New Yorkers start to unroll their column, he shouted to his own regiment, "Right by file into line!" The order was repeated, and he watched the regiment uncurl from marching column to fighting order with the rest of the brigade.

Arriving last, the 16th Michigan took up a position in the valley between the two hills on the far left. The 20th Maine was next, about twenty feet up a spur of the hill, its left flank resting in an open level space, and the rest of the 3rd Brigade line hugging the hill well below the summit. The shape of the rough, rocky ground created a bent line, causing the center of the 83rd Pennsylvania next to the 20th Maine to jut out a few feet. The line of the 44th New York ran up the slope toward the high part of the hill, its right resting in an open rocky area, with a clear view of the rock-strewn valley below. While the men moved into line, the reporter suddenly mounted his horse and rode away. Then a somber Vincent walked over to Lawrence.

"Colonel Chamberlain, there is going to be a desperate attack made over this ground. The enemy will probably try to turn our position and seize this hill. We will not let them do that. I want you to send out skirmishers so there will be no surprises. You are to hold this ground at all hazards."

"Yes, sir," Lawrence said. The order seemed simple enough. Then Vincent was gone, walking quickly to the other side of the hill.

Thomas was suddenly by the gelding's shoulder.

"Sir, the officers are sending their horses to the rear. I'll take yours." He quickly dismounted and handed Thomas the reins. Then he turned his attention to the regiment. As he walked past the right wing, he started thinking back on all those tactics books he read with Ames. He needed skirmishers out as ordered. He ran through the roster of company commanders in his mind and picked his most experienced, Walter Merrill and Company B, to fill the assignment. He knew Merrill was cool in an emergency. He would routinely bring a musket into battle so he could both shoot and command at the same time.

"Captain Merrill," he called, reaching the edge of Company B.

"Yes, sir," Merrill replied, musket in hand.

"I want you to take Company B out as skirmishers and hook up with the 16th Michigan's skirmish line. Keep within supporting distance of us and act as exigencies if the battle should require."

"Yes, sir." Merrill left, barking orders at Company B.

Lawrence watched them disappear in the thick foliage of the saddle between the hills, leaving his regiment forty rifles thinner. Then he noticed movement to his left. The 16th Michigan was leaving, appearing to be changing position and heading for the far right of the brigade line. It was too late to let Merrill know, but he had confidence the young captain would figure things out quickly and compensate. Far to the right, he could hear artillery fire and musketry that told of the desperate fight the 3rd Corps was continuing, but it was not close enough to affect them up on the spur.

He continued walking until he reached the color guard. He looked up and down his line. More nagging worries surfaced. This was going to be their first real stand-up fight. They were bone-tired from the forced march and largely untested. Only six of his ten companies were commanded by captains, and that had to be solved immediately. He spotted Ellis and Captain Atherton Clark by Company E on the right end talking to one another and went over to them.

"Gentlemen, as you know, we have no field officers. Ellis, I want you to watch over the left wing and Clark, you watch the right wing. Keep the men down. Have them pile up rocks or logs for some protection. When the shooting starts, have them aim low. Being on a hill, the tendency will be to shoot too high."

They nodded and quickly moved off to their new positions, passing orders to the company commanders. He continued to fret. Vincent was gone, out of sight, and God only knew if he'd see his

162

brigadier again once the shooting started in these shadowy woods. He could hardly see the 83rd Pennsylvania on his right through the trees, and the 16th Michigan was gone, leaving only rocks, trees, and Company B to hold back any Confederate attack from that direction. The haze of his lingering fever made him feel as if he were floating somewhere above himself, watching events unfold. He worried about his brothers and the more than four hundred men who now looked to him for guidance and survival itself on this brutally hot and humid Pennsylvania hillside. Worst of all, he felt as if the entire Rebel army was about to pounce on him and his small regiment from the foreboding woods in front of him.

Colonel Rice's voice startled him. "Will you join me for a minute to observe the approaching battle?" Rice asked.

"Yes, sir, I will," he said, feeling as though his conscious mind had been jerked back from a thousand miles away. They walked to a point below the brigade where they could see into the valley. All was a whirling, chaotic maelstrom.

The Confederates had turned the 3rd Corps left. A huge jumble of barn-sized boulders was wreathed in white smoke. A Union battery near the wheat field was being charged, while a large flanking force of the enemy was pushing toward the base of their hill and the big one next to it like a wave about to break on the shore. It was not the orderly horror of Fredericksburg, with men marching in straight battle lines to their slaughter. Here, chaos reigned in a shallow valley of death. A battery fired shot and shell, cutting a bloody, ragged chasm through a convulsing mass of men and screaming horses. A close-range musket volley sent a ragged battle line of men reeling in shock, muskets dropping, hands thrown in the air. Men writhed on the ground, while those not hit continued the fight, crouching amid the rocks for shelter from a terrible cross fire from which there was no safe haven. The whole wave of death and destruction advanced toward them in a powerful smoking force.

They looked at each other, both unable to find words. Then each quickly returned to their commands. Upon reaching his line, Lawrence immediately noticed the artillery had stopped. He did not feel much relief in this development as he walked toward the color company at the center of his line. He had learned from Ames that artillery simply cleared the way for infantry to follow, that shelling stopped when the attackers were too close for artillery to fire without hitting its own men. When a few hopeful faces turned his way, he called out, "They will be coming directly. Get ready."

He began to hear some high-pitched keening, moving toward them to the right. He recognized it instantly as the Rebel yell. It sent a chill through him, and he braced for the shock he knew would follow. His hand reached for the holster on his right hip to unbutton the flap, heart racing, breath coming short. Foliage to the right blocked his view of the oncoming Rebels.

With a scattering clatter of muskets, the assault was coming *en echelon*, hitting the 44th New York, then rolling like an ocean wave along the coast, heading right for them.

"Come to the ready," he called out, and the order was echoed along the line.

"Take good aim." Above them bullets began to clip twigs and cut branches, showering them with leaves. The bullets struck increasingly lower down the trunks and slapped into the rocks, sending small shards flying.

Lawrence took advantage of the little cover a six-inch diameter oak trunk provided. A bullet gouged a white furrow in it, sending splinters flying inches from his head, startling him. Another whistled past his ear. Then a few men were hit, doubled over, fell, one clutching a bloodied shoulder. The Rebel line rolled along about fifty yards out.

"Fire at will!" he yelled, aiming his pistol in the general direction of the enemy and pulling the trigger. The sharp report of his pistol was lost in a roar as the Maine line burst into a volley of flame and smoke. The enemy's formal battle line instantly disintegrated into an uneven collection of men among rocks and behind trees who began returning fire.

He quickly saw the Rebels were trying to cut up his line by fire rather than attempting to force the line in a charge. He could not stay where he was behind the oak. Walking behind his line only a few yards from the color guard, he felt his own fear and uncertainty boiling within but realized he must hold these emotions back, maintain his composure, and do so despite his inexperience, fever, and fatigue. He thought of how Ames was so cool under fire, knew how the men had looked to Ames for certainty at Fredericksburg in that futile assault on Marye's Heights. Now they looked to him. He must not fail them. Above the sporadic clatter of muskets he yelled loudly and firmly, "Boys, hold this hill!"

"We're gonna have a problem on the right. Clark can't find the end of the 83rd's line!" someone close by called over the shooting.

"Where the hell did Merrill get to? We'll need someone on the left." Ellis's voice barely reached him above the firing to the left.

Lieutenant James Nichols ran up to him. "Sir, there's something unusual happening behind the Rebs in front of my company. You better come see, sir."

Lawrence holstered his pistol and followed Nichols to the left behind the engaged line, dodging trees and rocks, ignoring the bullets that whistled past. He stopped with Nichols at Company K, looked around, and hopped up on a large boulder behind the middle of the company to see over the men and into the woods beyond. His breath caught in his throat at the sight of a thick group of the enemy moving toward his unprotected flank behind those engaged. They were now outnumbered two-to-one by the looks of it. He climbed off the rock to find Ellis next to Nichols.

"I can bend back two of my companies to cover the flank," Ellis shouted above the din.

"With what they are about to throw at us, we've got to do better than that," Chamberlain said. "Nichols, get Clark from over on the right wing and any of the other company commanders you can grab on the way."

Nichols ran off and quickly returned with Clark and Land.

"We are going to be flanked and have to move fast," Lawrence shouted over the din to the four officers with him. "I want the firing to be kept up on the enemy to disguise what we are about to do. Have the men in the right wing take side steps to the left when they can and stretch the line. I'm moving the colors to the new center. Ellis, you'll take the left wing and refuse the line at that point. We're going to be stretched thin in spots, but it should save our flank and give the enemy a nasty surprise. Do you all understand?"

They nodded and said, "Yes, sir."

"God be with you. Go!" he said.

They scattered to their commands. He headed for the color guard as orders went out, and the line slowly began to shift and stretch.

The second he reached the color guard, he called out, "Sergeant Tozier and the rest of you, come with me." They followed him to the extreme left where a rotted tree had fallen over. Its trunk, covered with moss and lichen, and a boulder ledge next to it made the position unassailable from the front. Taking a position about two dozen feet back from the ledge, he said, "This is your new position."

Then he saw Ellis and yelled, "Refuse the line here."

Masked from the flanking enemy, the men scrambled through brush and vines, around rocks and trees, some tripping and cursing as they took advantage of the cover and battle smoke. The line shifted under fire, forming a rough L shape around the crest of the rocky spur. He stood marveling how admirably the hazardous maneuver was carried out, knowing he had Ames to thank for the discipline that allowed it all to happen. Lawrence thought how proud

166

Ames would be if he could see them. The firing from the enemy slackened on the right.

"They're moving off down the hill," Thomas called as he ran toward Lawrence, finally catching up after taking the horse to the rear.

Lawrence turned toward the orderly. "Thomas, stay with …" He did not get the chance to finish his thought. At that instant, a bullet slammed into a rock by his right foot, and something hit his instep hard enough to trip him. Thomas grabbed him to keep him from falling. "Sir, you all right?"

He froze and looked down at his right foot. There was a small gash in his boot and a tiny trickle of blood. *No, not now, not here.* He put some weight on it. Pain shot up his leg. "I'll be all right. It must have been a rock fragment." He pulled the sword from the scabbard. "Can't let a scratch stop me. Stay close in case I need you."

"Yes, sir." Thomas said and fell in alongside, ducking twigs showering down from a tree next to them. Lawrence hobbled closer to the color guard, using the sword as a cane. The support helped take off some of the pressure, and the pain became a dull, annoying throb. "Here they come again!" Ellis yelled to his left. He and Thomas moved behind a couple of stout trees.

From where Lawrence stood, he could see a few men on his left running from rock to rock to find better cover as over two hundred gray- and butternut-clad troops walked, then rushed straight at what had been an exposed rear only moments before. The muzzles of more than a hundred Maine rifles blasted in a fiery volley that tore through the ranks of the horrified Confederates. They halted where they stood. This blow inflicted scores of casualties, suddenly evening the odds. When the Rebels recovered from the shock and returned fire, Lawrence and the rest of the men were grateful for the boulders and trees that provided protection. The brisk firing at close range forced the Confederates back among the low trees and rocks

167

of the valley. Some of them took up a position among rocks below the left wing and began an effective fire that created havoc. Many of the Maine men on the left were forced to scramble back to the shelter of larger rocks and trees, where they held. Then the Rebels burst forth again with a yell, firing as they came. But the galling fire from the left wing compelled them to break and take cover again. Lawrence could see both sides had settled in for a prolonged fight in the deepening forest shadows.

In many places, the lines were only seventy feet apart, and the roar of the muskets was so loud it drowned out the commands of the officers. He observed many of his men dumping their cartridges out in easy reach and sticking the ramrods into the ground between shots, making it very plain they did not intend to be driven back. Through battle smoke as thick as fog, Ellis ran over to him.

"Sir, my line is scattered because of the ground. The enemy has crept forward and is firing from behind boulders by the ledge. I'm afraid they're going to overlap my left. Something's got to be done, sir. Could you possibly send over two companies from the right?"

"I'll go over and see what I can do, Ellis," he replied. Ellis nodded and disappeared in the smoke. He turned and limped toward the right wing, with Thomas right beside him. Bullets whistled by, too close, and hit the trees around him. Men were dropping. Some were heading back to the aid station. As he reached the right wing, it seemed to not be as heavily engaged. He went to Companies E and I, found Captain Fogler and Lieutenant Linscott, their commanders. "Fogler, Linscott, take your companies off the line and go reinforce the left wing," he yelled. Orders were shouted. The two companies began to fall back toward the left and nearly created a stampede for the rear, though Company K, the third in line, held their ground, looking confused. This move was a bad mistake, a serious lapse of judgment. "No! Halt!" Lawrence yelled, waving his sword. This was not going to work in the confusion of combat. "I countermand the order!" Captain Clark joined him and yelled, "For

Christ's sake, get back in line! Move it! Move it!" The companies returned to their original positions and continued to fire into the withdrawing enemy. As much as he hated to, he knew it was best to leave Ellis and the left wing to their own devices. He had faith that Ellis would hold on any way he could. Through the drifts of battle smoke to his right, a young lieutenant he did not know came running toward him, dodging rocks and fallen men.

"Colonel, sir," the lieutenant yelled once he was close enough. "I'm Adjutant Gifford of the 83rd." He quickly saluted and it was returned. "We had bullets come over our heads from the rear. Captain Woodward, our commander, sent me to see if the 20th had broken."

"Well, Lieutenant, we haven't yet. But we could sure use the aid of a company or two if you can spare them," he said.

"I'll see what we can do, sir." The lieutenant ran off into the smoke, dodging and ducking as trees were hit around him.

Lawrence hobbled toward the left to check on Ellis. Immediately, another assault hit. This time the yelling Rebels surged forward to seize the spur, slamming into the center and right of his line, the attack itself taking the form of chaotic brawls, often between two men swinging rifles, bayonets, or even fists. Peripherally, he saw Thomas a few yards to his left fire his rifle quickly, then swing it to block and fend off a bayonet attack by a young Rebel. He turned in time to see Thomas deftly bring the rifle butt up sharply against the youth's head and drop him in a twitching heap. He turned away and kept heading left. *Don't think. Don't look too close. Keep moving.* The 20th held, and the Rebels withdrew down the slope to regroup, a few continuing to fire as they went.

In the lull, he caught sight of Lieutenant Gifford scrambling back through the rocks and drifting smoke in the pools of the late afternoon sun that filtered through the scarred trees.

169

"Sir," he panted upon catching up. "Captain Woodward regrets we cannot spare any men, but he will extend his line to yours, and this should provide some relief."

"Good. Tell him that will be much appreciated," he said.

"I will, sir." The lieutenant scrambled away again.

Thomas caught up. He had recovered from the bayonet attack as if nothing had happened. "We're starting to run low on ammunition, sir. Thought you should know."

"Send a couple of runners to the rear and right to see what you can get up here. See if anyone else in the brigade can spare us a company."

"Yes, sir."

Lawrence watched Thomas run along the line and pull out a couple of men. The drifting smoke blanketed the scene. He paused, leaning on the hilt of his sword, and wiped the sweat out of his eyes with his coat sleeve. He looked out at the depleted regiment. It was an exaggeration to call it a battle line. Men, individuals and in groups, were scattered behind every available tree, rock, pile of logs, or rise in the ground that made a useful or safe position from which to fire. He knew the officers left could hardly tell where their company lines began or ended. In any further attacks like this last one, commands would be almost useless in the noise and confusion. Tactics by the book would be virtually impossible. This whole fight was quickly coming down to scattered groups of men doing what they could to hold the spur. All he could hope for was to keep moving and hold his regiment together. He continued limping toward the colors, past the groups of men taking cover and the stretcher bearers removing the fallen. Many looked momentarily over their shoulders at him. "Keep it up, boys. We'll hold them off. You're doing fine," he said to encourage them.

Movement in the woods out in front of them caught his eye.

170

"Christ, you'd think they'd have learned their lesson by now." He heard Captain Land's foghorn voice rise above the first shots of another assault.

The scattered shots from both sides quickly became deadly volleys as the Rebels pressed home another charge. He saw the rough lines collide in confusion and hand-to-hand fighting. Maine men swung rifles like axes, crushing skulls with a sickening crack. A few close shots by Confederates took more men down. A soldier no more than eighteen ran past him for better cover and was shot down. When he went to the boy, he saw spreading blood on the shirt and the light of life leaving his eyes. It sobered him to think the boy had unknowingly taken a bullet meant for him. A fog of battle smoke drifted around him. Violent shadows grappled; gray forms cut their way through dark blue forms. He saw more of the enemy around him than his own troops. His men were being forced from their original position. On the rocks, blood stood in puddles. On the ground, the wounded of both sides called for help. Men prayed or sang snatches of Sabbath songs or cursed. Just as suddenly, the gray forms drifted back down the hill, firing as they backed away.

Sergeant Thomas reached him. "Sir, no one can spare any ammunition, and the whole brigade has been having a hot time of it on the other side of this hill. Heard Vincent's down," the sergeant panted.

"Vincent down?" Lawrence found himself repeating in disbelief.

"Don't know any details, sir. The other men I sent couldn't get help either."

Tom came over, pistol in hand. "I ain't had any better luck, and our left wing is about out of ammunition."

"Go back along the line and tell them to get cartridges from the boxes of the dead and wounded," he said. "Let's hope we won't be at this much longer. They've got to be as tired as we are."

"Let's hope so, sir," Thomas said. Both men left.

Lawrence limped past the colors to the beleaguered left wing. The men were taking cartridges from the dead and wounded and dropping their Enfields in favor of the more reliable Springfields among the fallen Rebels, both in front and to the rear of their line. Others were piling up more logs and stones to provide better shelter. Among them, he found a soldier who had received a severe wound across his forehead. Lewis was with him, helping him to stand. With prompt medical attention, he felt the soldier might survive or at least die in peace at the field hospital.

"Lewis, see if you can get him back to the aid station."

"Consider it done, sir," Lewis said, helping the man move off to the rear.

He continued hobbling toward the left of his regiment, passing Company H, checking the men.

He came upon Private George Washington Buck, the young sergeant the bullying quartermaster had wrongly demoted in winter camp. Buck was sitting on the ground, his back leaning against a tree. He had his coat open and was bleeding badly from a wound in his right shoulder. There was little doubt in Lawrence's mind about the young soldier's fate. A major artery had been hit or nicked. Buck's eyes focused on him and reached out a blood-stained hand. Lawrence knelt beside him. "My dear boy, it has gone hard with you. You will be cared for."

Buck struggled to reply in almost a whisper. "Tell my mother … I did not die a coward."

Deeply moved, he felt his own throat go tight. "You die a sergeant. I promote you for faithful service and noble courage on the field of Gettysburg!" A couple of stretcher bearers arrived at that moment, gently lifted the sergeant to the stretcher, and carried him to the rear.

He stood slowly and watched them leave, feeling emotionally drained. The firing began anew, and the Confederates started up the hill again, the slaughter resuming along the left. In the confusion of smoke and embattled soldiers, he spotted Captain Land not far from Ellis, helping him keep the line intact. In front of Land, Sergeant Isaac Lathrop, the easily recognizable six-foot giant of Company H, suddenly doubled over, hit in the stomach, and went down. Right next to him the first sergeant of the company, Charles Steele, managed to stagger up to Land despite a severe chest wound. "My God, Sergeant Steele!" Land's voice boomed.

"I am gone," Steele replied and dropped dead at Land's feet.

"Pour it into them!" Ellis yelled, and a return volley exploded from the shrinking line. Increased fire from the center drew Lawrence's attention, and he turned to hobble back in that direction.

He found a desperate yet inspiring scene. The two companies on either side of the colors had been badly cut up by the Confederates at the foot of the spur. From what he could see through the battle smoke, hardly a platoon was left to hold the center. Bullets still tore through them in three directions. When some of the smoke drifted away, he glimpsed Color Sergeant Tozier. The sergeant had the staff of the colors firmly planted in the ground at his side, the upper part clamped in the crook of his elbow as he fired a musket with cartridges taken from a fallen comrade at his side. All the while, he coolly chewed a piece of cartridge paper as he fired.

Tom and Sergeant Thomas appeared through the smoke, back from their mission. "Tom, go fill that hole," Lawrence yelled, pointing at the colors, and saw Tom turn and run for the center. Realizing suddenly that his brother would probably not reach the center alive, he looked at Thomas. "Go help him."

The sergeant ran after him.

He watched for a moment, his feverish mind slowing his reactions. He must do something. *Move, fool, before you are overrun.* He drew his pistol and fired at the shadowy forms of the enemy moving toward him in the drifting smoke, hobbling along as the center of his line pulled back under tremendous pressure to a stronger position. He saw one Rebel drop, felt no remorse or anger,

173

only a will to survive. Other men from surrounding companies helped fill the gap, soon masked by smoke from the continuous firing. He looked through breaks in the smoke and, to his horror, saw the Confederates had the spur. The assault unexpectedly stalled. They could not keep it and began to slip down into the valley. He holstered the pistol, turned, and limped toward the right, also under a steady heavy fire. He had not gone far when something slammed into his left thigh with the force of a mule kick, knocking him down hard and stunning him.

Suddenly, two men were bending over him. He looked up and seemed to be focusing through fog. It was Tom and Captain Clark.

"Are you hit, sir?" Clark asked.

His senses came back. *You've been shot, fool. No, I can't go down. Not now.*

"I don't know," he said thickly and slowly sat up, feeling along his thigh with his hand. The steel scabbard of the sword hanging from his belt was bent. He touched the point of impact on his thigh and flinched at the pain, but there was no wound. The bullet had hit the scabbard and bent it against his leg, leaving it badly bruised, but he was all right.

"I'll be damned," he said and held up the scabbard. He moved to get up but was unsteady.

"You're damned lucky, sir," Clark said as he and Tom took him under an arm and hauled him to his feet.

"Lord, you gave me a fright," Tom added.

They continued along the embattled right wing. Lawrence limped with a new source of pain and started wondering if any of them were going to get off this hill alive.

Tom and Clark went ahead, disappearing in the thick drifts of battle smoke. Lawrence kept hobbling along behind the embattled men on the right wing, thinking of Ames, trying to provide the confidence he knew his men needed to hold on, while trying just as desperately not to let his pain, fatigue, or inexperience show.

The shooting began to slacken. This attack had fallen shorter than the others on the right. The smoke was clearing from the crest of the hill, and he finally got a good look at what was left of his command in the deepening shadows. He could easily see the last assault had been the fiercest. Half the left wing was down, and half the men he had brought to the spur were no longer in their places. There was no way on God's earth they were going to hold off another enemy attack like the last one.

Some of the men glanced back at him with beseeching looks on their sweaty, powder-stained faces. Others grabbed the hot barrels of their muskets and prepared to use them as clubs. Still others busied themselves with piling up more rocks or with one last desperate search through the cartridge boxes of the fallen.

"Sir, I'm out of ammunition," called one man with a bloody rag tied around his head.

"Me, too, sir," said another.

"I got only a couple of rounds left," someone else called from down the line.

Their words and looks told him they needed him to tell them now, at their most desperate hour, what to do to make it through this hell.

Tom came up. "Colonel, we're totally out of ammunition on the right and not much better on the left. Thomas is back at the aid station. He took one in the shoulder in that attack on the center."

A sudden roar of muskets off to the rear on the far slope of the hill increased his anxiety. Bullets appeared to be hitting among the beleaguered left wing from that fight. He feared all was lost on the other side and that the Union batteries were about to be turned against him from the rear at any moment.

175

In front of him, the dead and wounded of both sides mingled on the bloody ground. Beyond them down the slope, he could just see the enemy through the woods, rallying for what looked like another assault. He thought about Vincent's last order to hold his position at all hazards. How was that possible now?

Then he remembered a passage from Jomini's *The Art of War*. "When the assailant, after suffering severely, finds himself strongly assailed at the moment when victory seemed to be in his hands, the advantage will, in all probability, be his no longer, for the moral effect of such a counter-attack upon the part of an adversary supposed to be beaten is certainly enough to stagger the boldest troops."

Then more words surfaced. "The best thing for an army standing on the defensive is to know *how* to take the offensive at the proper time, and *to take it*."

The only practical option he had was to order a charge down into the Rebels and hope to scatter them before they charged again. They had to be as tired and thirsty as his own men by now. The only weapon left for most of the men was the bayonet, eighteen inches of cold steel, and the psychological effect it would have that was an edge as keen as the steel itself.

The bent-back left wing would have to be notified. Before he could do so, Lieutenant Holman Melcher of Company F, one of the badly shot-up color companies, came out of the drifting smoke from the left, spotted him, and ran over.

"Sir," Lieutenant Melcher said, "I've come to ask permission to advance the center to retrieve our wounded out in front. Most of them can't move far and have been calling out to us for help."

He admired Melcher's bravery and compassion. "Lieutenant, you will have help. I am about to order a charge. Return to your company."

Melcher stared at him in disbelief for a second, nodded, and ran off toward the center. He hobbled to the right of Tozier, Elisha Coan

176

and William Livermore, all that were left of the color guard. Competing with the din of the battle from the other side of the hill, he took a deep breath, raised his sword, and yelled as loudly as he could, "Bayonet!"

Other officers took up the call, echoing it down the line. Steel rang as men pulled their bayonets and fastened them to their musket barrels. A loud, hoarse cheer rose from many throats, almost drowning out his yell of, "Forward!" He took a step, pointing his sword down the hill at the drifting smoke and moving shadows in the brush and among the rocks. The line tentatively started to move.

Melcher ran ahead a few feet, waving his sword and shouting, "Come on! Come on, men!"

The men of the right wing were suddenly running down the spur, the wild charge taking up an impetus all its own. Sword up, he hobbled as fast as he could, staying with Tozier and the color guard descending the hill in the lead. He hoped the shouted orders of officers down the line would alert Ellis to start the left wing on a similar course. *Ellis will certainly start moving as soon as he sees the colors heading down the hill through the trees.*

As they hit the Rebel line, many of the enemy threw down their rifles and cried out, "Don't fire! We surrender!"

The rest began to flee in wild confusion, some off to the right and some up toward the big hill on the left.

He saw Elisha Coan rush ahead of him, gather five prisoners and head them up the hill to the rear at bayonet point. When the charge reached the ledge, the line divided because of the steep drop. He and the colors went to the right of it, while some of Melcher's company paused to help the wounded. Just past the ledge, the wild charge started to meet resistance.

Some of the Confederates stopped to take a few final shots at their pursuers. A young lieutenant stood suddenly. He waited calmly for perhaps ten seconds. In those seconds, the officers examined each other with the unblinking scrutiny of those who take chances.

177

Lawrence painfully tried to slow his momentum down the slope. When he got within six feet of the lieutenant, he suddenly found a big Colt pistol aimed squarely at his face. He could do little more than brace himself for the fatal shot.

The pistol went off, missing him despite the close range. Breathing the acrid smoke of the discharge, he knocked the pistol out of the way with his sword, drawing the point to the lieutenant's neck, and stood there, his heart hammering in his chest.

Eyes still defiant, the young officer slowly handed over his pistol and sword with the words, "I am your prisoner, sir." With the shock of the encounter quickly melting, he had the luxury of admiring the lieutenant's courage.

When a sergeant drew up even with him, he called out, "Sergeant, take the lieutenant to the rear. See to it that nothing happens to him." The sergeant tucked the pistol in his belt, knowing he could always use an extra sidearm.

As the sergeant started up the hill with the prisoner, Lawrence continued after the regiment. He heard firing to the left and saw Ellis bringing the left wing swinging around even with the right. Beyond them more bluecoats were firing into the fleeing enemy. It could only be Merrill and the lost Company B. He thought he saw green uniforms among them and realized they must have met a unit of the US sharpshooters. Smoke suddenly blotted out the scene.

Some of the men who had charged ahead of him were shouting, "We're on our way to Richmond!"

He continued after them. Looking up at the smaller rocky hill, he determined they were about even with the position of the 44th New York in a portion of the shallow valley littered with wounded men from the frontal attack on the hill. The firing slackened and died away to occasional scattered reports. *We have gone far enough.* He knew the Rebels who had taken cover among the rocks and trees of the big hill and those who were still in the valley ahead could do great damage to what was left of his regiment if they rallied. With that thought came the realization he was technically in violation of his orders to hold the ground. That proved an equal incentive to get back up the hill to the rocky spur.

He saw Clark to his right with a lieutenant and yelled, "Captain Clark, tell every officer you meet to get the men back to our original position."

"Yes, sir," Clark yelled back.

Tom came barreling past, pistol in one hand and sword in the other.

"Tom, pass the word. Get the men back to our original position on that spur," he called after him.

"Yes, sir!" Tom yelled, nearly slamming into a tree as he ran. He changed direction to run parallel to the charging men, yelling, "Back up the hill, boys! It's over! Richmond can wait!"

Slowly, the mad charge petered out as the officers got control and the men started back toward the spur with prisoners at bayonet point. He saw some of the men rally around the tattered colors and give three cheers. Tozier had a broad grin on his powder-smeared face and was still chewing cartridge paper. Next to him, Livermore was grinning, too, and called to him, "Colonel, can you beat this? We face the Rebs head-on the first time in a real fight, and we whipped them!"

Lawrence forced a smile and nodded, suddenly too tired and overheated to feel much like celebrating. The smoke was clearing behind them, and the confusion was subsiding. He started painfully hobbling up the slope. It was all he could do to keep moving one foot in front of the other over the steep rocky ground. He had not gone far when in the fading light he noticed a high-ranking Confederate officer with white hair and goatee sitting under a tree. The man had to be in his sixties. He limped over to the officer, found he was in serious condition, lung shot, with blood still seeping from the wound and his mouth.

The officer focused on him, defiance still in his eyes and croaked, "I am Lieutenant Colonel Bulger ... 47th Alabama, Colonel."

"I'll send someone back for you. Do not move or you may further injure yourself," he said and hobbled on.

He stopped a corporal. "Back at that tree is Colonel Bulger of the 47th Alabama. He's seriously wounded. Get the stretcher bearers to take him to the rear."

"Yes, sir," the corporal said and moved on.

As he continued limping up the slope in the growing twilight, the cost of this victory suddenly became all too clear. Dead and wounded from both sides lay among the rocks and trees around the spur from top to bottom. Blood stood in dark puddles on the rocks and low spots on the ground around them. Trees were scarred up to six feet, and a few up to three inches in diameter had been cut down by bullets. The wounded who had not been taken to the aid station were now being gathered up with the bodies. On the way to the center where the colors had stood, he estimated about one hundred fifty enemy dead and wounded lay along the line. As he reached the center with what was left of the color guard and companies, he realized the gravity of it all, noting here, where the colors stood in the fight, forty-eight of his men had been killed or wounded.

Struggling to catch his breath from the climb, Lawrence watched the exhausted, sweaty survivors following him up the slope, pushing along prisoners at bayonet point, most with their rifles empty. Strange feelings churned within him—a bittersweet mix of guilt for surviving; remorse over those who did not; sorrow, joy, and most of all, a sense of deep relief that came with such a desperate victory.

Slowly, in the deepening twilight, most of what was left of the regiment collected itself along their original position. He called a halt, and many not occupied with prisoners or wounded sank down where they stood and fell asleep on their arms. He found himself looking off through the trees and brush at the dark, brooding slope of the larger hill. He suspected the fight for the spur was over but knew the dark forested slope of the big hill held the Confederates who had gotten away during the charge. If they reformed or got reinforcements, he knew it would mean more trouble than his small exhausted regiment could handle, maybe more than what was left of the brigade could handle.

———⊰•⊱———

Lawrence sat on a low boulder to get the weight off his throbbing foot after walking the line, counting his men, and seeing that the wounded were tended. He stared at the leaf litter at his feet, trying to comprehend everything he had just been through. A twig snapped. He looked up. Tom walked to him out of the nearly dark woods.

"Lord, what a mess this all is," Tom said, sitting next to him. "Sure you don't want to see a doctor about your foot?"

"For a scratch? I'd be mortified. They have enough on their hands with real wounds," he returned, wondering briefly how John was doing with the aid station.

"Well, I found out a lot wandering around, helping with the wounded all over this hill. Talked to some fellers from the 83rd. As hard as we had it on this spur, I think the rest of the brigade had it just as bad … maybe worse. Lord Almighty, the news is real bad about most of our commanders over there. Damn Rebel snipers had themselves a field day in that pile of boulders they call Devil's Den. Colonel Vincent has been mortally wounded."

"No!" The shock hit like a physical blow. He had known Vincent was down but did not want to believe it. Not Vincent.

"Yes, I'm afraid so. He went down in the very beginning of the fight, from what Captain Woodward said. Colonel Rice now has our brigade. We lost General Weed, Lieutenant Hazlett, even Colonel

181

O'Rorke of the 140th New York, who came just in time to stop a disaster on the right … all …" He paused, choked with emotion, and shook his head, unable to go further.

They sat in dismal silence. Lawrence was aware of crickets chirping in the brush. An owl called. Nature's creatures carried on as if nothing had happened.

Tom continued. "I talked to some of the boys. I don't think a single man in our regiment was not hit by enemy fire in some way or another, even if it was just through their clothes or blanket roll. Only three of our captains remain in command of their companies. Captain Sam Keene of Company F is still on his feet, though. When you sent me and Thomas to help in the center, I saw him go down. He's plenty sore. Bullet hit his sword belt and bruised his hip real bad." He paused to wipe sweat from his forehead with his sleeve. "The regiments we fought were the 15th and 47th Alabama. Some of the prisoners are from Texas, too. According to Will Livermore in the color guard, one of the prisoners from the 15th Alabama told him they ain't never been whipped before and never want to fight the 20th Maine again."

"Any idea how many men we have left fit for duty? I counted one hundred and ninety-eight," he said hoarsely. "That includes Captain Merrill and Company B down on the skirmish line below the base of the big hill."

"The company commanders are still trying to compile casualty lists. Between stragglers, men helping the wounded, burial details, and details out seeking ammunition, I'd say you are close."

A fear settled cold in his gut, an old fear of being exposed and vulnerable. "That's hardly a strong skirmish line and certainly not enough to defend this spur. The Alabama regiments are still on that big hill in front of us. We could have real trouble again by morning if not sooner."

"Don't I know it," Tom said. "But the dark at least might make them cautious. What do you want me to tell the company commanders?"

"In case the worst comes, have the wounded prisoners taken to the rear and gather our dead in an area behind our line. It would also be a good idea to have the men pile up more rocks."

"Yes, sir." Tom stood up slowly.

As Tom walked away, another officer came out of the gloom of the deepening twilight.

"Colonel Chamberlain?" He saluted.

"Yes," he said, not recognizing the man.

"Colonel Rice sent me to find you, sir. He would like to see you."

Lawrence got up painfully, the inaction and easing of battle tension bringing out all the aches with a vengeance. "Lead on," he said, limping after the officer, continuing to use his sword as a cane.

As he hobbled along, he felt shaky with a mix of fever and fatigue. He hoped no one would notice in the dark. Colonel Rice was over by the 44th New York, the regiment at rest around him. He saw small fires scattered along the ridge and smelled coffee boiling. "Sir, you sent for me," he said and saluted.

"Colonel Chamberlain, your gallantry was magnificent, and your coolness and skill saved us."

"Thank you, sir, but the credit must go to the men. They performed remarkably well," he said. "And I must not overlook the help from Adjutant Gifford and Captain Woodward."

"You are too modest, Colonel. You know Colonel Vincent is not expected to live?"

"Yes, sir. I will miss him." He looked at the ground, feeling his throat go tight with emotion. *Control. This is not the time to let a numbing grief take over.* He promised himself to write Vincent's wife, Elizabeth, to see she was taken care of.

Rice sighed. "We all will miss him, Colonel. I do have some welcome news, for all it's worth. I have brought up reinforcements from another part of the corps. Colonel Joseph Fisher's Brigade of Pennsylvania Reserves and three thousand rounds of ammunition are on the way." Rice paused, staring at the ground a moment. He looked up and continued. "I am extremely uncomfortable about what the Rebels might be up to on Wolf Hill, as I know you are. I asked Colonel Fisher to occupy the hill with his brigade. He declined on the grounds that his men have just arrived and are ignorant of the situation. Thus, it would be dangerous in the dark. Be that as it may, do you think you can carry that hill? This is not a direct order, Colonel. I know you and your regiment have already done more than expected … more than anyone could imagine when this fight started. But you have had experience with night maneuvers at Fredericksburg. No one will hold it against you if you decline, Colonel."

He offered no comment on Fisher's refusal but knew Wolf Hill had to be secured before daylight. "I will see what can be done," he returned, knowing he had to figure out a way to tell his exhausted men they had to climb a hill infested with the enemy in the dark.

"Thank you, Colonel. I'll await word of your progress and will get you some support," Rice said.

On his way back, he noticed the full moon was up. The silver light sent a few shafts through the leafy canopy, settling in pools on the forest floor. All but a few pickets were asleep on their arms. He looked at his depleted line and did not have the heart to order them up. He limped on to the colors. Tozier was awake, as were Livermore and Coan. They were talking in low tones but stopped and gave him their full attention when he paused by them. A few men near them stirred, looked up, and poked others awake around them.

"Boys, I am asked if we can carry this hill in front," he started. "I am going, and the colors will follow me. As many of you as feel able to do so can follow us. There will be no shooting. Use the bayonet if need be. We cannot risk an engagement that will reveal just how small our numbers are."

Sword in hand, he limped toward the foreboding bigger hill. He could hear men stirring, following. He looked over his shoulder, and in the patches of moonlight, he saw every one of them stand up. Officers moved in the gloom, trimming up the formation.

Tom came over.

"Tom, get word to Captain Merrill out on the skirmish line to join us," he said.

"Yes, sir," Tom replied and was gone.

Lawrence continued, straining to see in the dark. An occasional shot from a nervous picket in the far distance broke the silence. He heard Company B arrive and take its place. Cautiously, he entered the dark woods at the base of Wolf Hill. In the best battle line they could manage over the rough ground, the regiment advanced. Moonlight filtering through the branches did little to relieve the blackness. Soon he found his eyes becoming accustomed to the dark.

They pushed forward. Something small ran through the brush. Someplace in the murky darkness nervous Southerners began to fire at real or imagined noises. Bullets harmlessly clipped leaves and branches overhead. The sudden, explosive whistling sound of beating mourning dove wings startled him. Just before they reached the top of the hill, there was a disturbance on their left. Some of the men captured a half dozen Confederates, including an officer from General Law's staff. Once at the top, he could hear noise below that indicated the enemy was close and in force directly in front of them. He turned to Tom, who was close by. "Pass the word to the company commanders to have the men take cover. Have Captain Merrill take Company B down the hill in a skirmish line to keep an eye on things. I want to know what's down there. How big a force."

"Yes, sir." Tom went stumbling off along the line on his mission.

Lawrence heard the skirmishers move away and checked his pocket watch in a pool of moonlight. It was 9:45. He waited by a tree, thinking dismal thoughts of Southern prison camps or worse while the rest of the regiment huddled around him behind rocks and trees in their exposed position. Time passed by interminably slowly.

There was noise in the woods ahead, movement through brush, the rattle of equipment. His heart pounded. He could feel the fever begin its burn, knew he was pushing himself to the limit. He also knew if they were all captured, he would never survive prison. It chilled him to envision Fannie in black. *How many of the others are having such thoughts? What was I thinking dragging my exhausted regiment up an enemy-infested hill in the dark? Duty? Rice himself said they had all done more than what was expected of them.* The sound of men pushing through brush closer in front stopped his growing pangs of regret.

A voice challenged, "Halt! Who goes there?"

"Merrill, Company B. We got thirty prisoners," came the answer from Captain Merrill. "All of them Texans from Hood's Division not three hundred yards down the hill." The words were no sooner out of his mouth when noise from a large force crashing through the brush and clattering over rocks erupted in their rear, cutting them off from the brigade.

"Prepare for an attack!" Lawrence called and heard his own men shift position in the dark as he ducked behind a large boulder and, with painful difficulty, knelt on the ground.

"Oh, hell! It's those Pennsylvanian Reserves," Land boomed from the edge of the line. "They're coming up the hill by the left flank. God, what a bunch of idiots. They're going to end up with their butts to the enemy when they halt. Holy Mother of God! Now they're trying to correct it!" The attempt digressed into a noisy mess, judging by the sound of the crash of brush and curses.

A Confederate far down the hill yelled, "Fire!"

186

A volley shattered the night, harmlessly passing over the regiment, clipping twigs and leaves, sending them down in a softly rustling shower. The crashing in the brush and the shouting suddenly receded down the hill behind them. The night's forest silence closed in.

"Captain Merrill, send out a few of your men as a picket line to our rear. We don't need any more surprises," he called.

"Yes, sir," Merrill replied as Tom returned.

"Tom, get word to Colonel Rice we've got the hill but need some reliable help holding it." Tom nodded and was gone.

He waited in the dark listening, praying the Texans below would not figure out how few blue-clad troops they really faced. He did not know how long he waited, even caught himself dozing as he leaned against the boulder. The snap of brush ended his slumber and told him a large force of troops was approaching. Anxiety gripped him. His heart thumped coldly. He stood, felt the Colt in his belt, and started to reach for it.

Out of the dark a young officer appeared in front of him, the moonlight glinting on captain's bars. "Colonel Chamberlain, sir, is that you?" he asked.

"Yes."

"I'm Captain Woodward of the 83rd. Colonel Rice sent us and the 44th New York, now coming up behind us, to support you."

"That's the best news I've had all night," he said, grinning with relief.

"The Pennsylvania Reserves will be following come daylight. They seem a little shaken by their first attempt to climb this hill."

"They made quite a mess of the whole affair and were so noisy they drew fire," he explained, watching the reinforcements take up position. "I'm going to have my boys get what sleep they can. They are all played out. Let me know every half hour what the status is. I'm going to try to get a little sleep myself."

"Yes, sir." Woodward saluted and left.

Lawrence eased down against a boulder to sit, with his sore leg and foot out in front of him, the sword at his side, the bent scabbard useless. He drew deep into his thoughts. *How much longer would this slaughter go on before the South understood they could not win?*

He looked into the dark forest and thought of the desperate fight for the spur, of Vincent and his men languishing in field hospitals, and the dead being buried behind the hill. He made a promise to himself he would go to the hospitals and check on them as soon as he could.

His thoughts raced on to what they had accomplished beyond the glory and suffering. The regiment had passed the trial by fire in their first stand-up fight at great cost. He had proven he could command in the crisis of combat. Beyond that, maybe they had helped bring the Union that much closer to a final victory and reuniting the torn and bleeding country.

But there was much more on a deeper level.

In great deeds something abides. On great fields something stays. Forms change and pass; bodies disappear; but spirits linger, to consecrate ground for the vision-place of souls. And reverent men and women from afar, and generations that know us not and we know not of, heart-drawn to see where and by whom great things were suffered and done for them, shall come to this deathless field, to ponder and dream; and lo! the shadow of a mighty presence shall wrap them in its bosom, and the power of the vision pass into their souls.

Joshua Lawrence Chamberlain

Milton Keynes UK
Ingram Content Group UK Ltd.
UKHW042002291124
451915UK00004B/390